Contents

CHAPTER I

Packing

"ONLY one day more," cried Patty Hirst, surveying with deep interest the large new box which stood by the side of the chest of drawers in her bedroom; "just one day! How dreadfully quickly the time has come! I feel quite queer when I think about it. I can scarcely believe that before the end of the week both I and my luggage will be a whole hundred miles away, and settled at Morton Priory. I do wonder how I shall like it?"

"Very much, I hope," replied her mother, pausing for a moment in her task of packing the neat piles of linen and underclothing into as small a compass as possible. "I'm sure it seems a delightful school, and you are an extremely lucky girl to be going there."

"Yes," said Patty, with a rather doubtful tone in her voice, sitting down on the edge of the bed, and beginning to turn over the pocket handkerchiefs, the new blouses, the ties, hair ribbons, and other articles which made up her schoolgirl outfit; "I suppose I am lucky. Perhaps it may be nicer than I think. I wanted to go dreadfully when Uncle Sidney first wrote about it, but somehow now that it's got almost to starting off, do you know I feel as if I'd changed my mind, and I'm not at all sure that I wouldn't rather stay at home. It seems too horrible to have to go amongst so many new girls."

Mrs. Hirst laughed.

"Don't be a silly child," she said. "Of course you will feel strange just at first, but you will soon get over your shyness. It will be quite a fresh world for you, and a very interesting one. I expect to have the most enthusiastic letters from you when you have been there for a few weeks."

"It will be different from Miss Dawson's, at any rate," said Patty.

"I hope it will. Miss Dawson's is the best school we have in Kirkstone, but it is only moderately good. I can't be too glad for you to have this opportunity of going to a better one. Give me your stockings, dear, and the workbasket; I've a corner I want to fill up here."

Patty sat watching her mother's deft fingers in silence for a moment or two, only handing her from time to time the things which she required. She gave a little sigh of satisfaction as she saw all her belongings stowed away in the big box; she had never had so many new possessions in her life before, and in the pleasure of owning them felt some slight compensation for the wrench of parting from home. The two useful navy-blue serge skirts, with their accompanying blouses, the pretty brown velvet dress for Sundays, the flowered delaine for evenings, and the white muslin for school parties, not to mention the hats, coats, and the numberless small articles needed for a girl going away by herself, all represented much thought and some self-denial on the part of her mother, who had made a great effort to send her nicely equipped, and had toiled hard to finish everything in time.

"I don't believe anybody could have a prettier nightdress case or brush-and-comb bag than this," said Patty, proudly smoothing the lace edging which she had helped to stitch on herself; "and the clothes bag is a perfect beauty. Here's the little cash-box, Mother. It seems such a funny thing to have to take to school. I haven't any 'valuables' to put into it, except my pocket money, and you said Miss Lincoln would take care of that. Why must it have two keys?"

"In case you lose one, I suppose. No doubt Miss Lincoln is well accustomed to schoolgirls' careless ways. You can keep your brooches inside it, and your locket and chain. Now give me your serviette ring and your collars, and don't forget that I've put the boot laces in your workbasket."

"I wonder if I shall unpack by myself, or if anyone will come to help me," said Patty.

"You'll soon find out what is expected, and of course Muriel will be able to tell you everything. It's so very nice for you to have your cousin at the school. You'll have a friend there already."

Patty's face fell.

"I'm not sure, Mother," she said, rather hesitatingly. "The truth is, I'm afraid Muriel doesn't want me to go. She was so queer and offhand about it when I was staying at Thorncroft; she wouldn't talk of it at all, though Aunt Lucy did. Somehow I think she won't like me to be at the same school as herself."

"You must be mistaken, dear! Why, Uncle Sidney was so pleased with his project, and said you were to take care of Muriel as if she were your sister."

"I know he did; but all the same, I don't believe Muriel herself will like it. She's never been very fond of me; Horace is always much jollier when I go there. When Aunt Lucy said she hoped we should both be in the same class, Muriel looked quite cross, and said of course I should be lower down, as she had gone to school first, and girls who were in different forms scarcely saw anything of each other; and then, when we were out in the garden together, she said she didn't see why I must be sent to The Priory, and surely there were other schools I could have gone to."

"Never mind, dear! Perhaps she was a little out of temper that day, and may prove nicer when you really arrive. You must try to keep friends with her, even if she's not always quite pleasant. We mustn't forget Uncle Sidney's kindness. I feel very grateful to him, for we couldn't possibly have sent you to such an expensive school on our own account."

"I'll try," said Patty, "as far as she'll let me. If she were more like Milly it would be much easier. Oh! how dreadfully I shall miss you and Father, and Basil, and the little ones! I wish I could go to school and take my family with me. I don't know how I'm to manage for thirteen whole weeks without once seeing any of you. The time will never go by."

"Poor little woman!" said her mother. "It does seem hard, I know, but you must look forward to meeting us all again, and the days will pass much faster than you imagine."

"But, Mother darling, you'll have so much to do while I'm away. Who'll help you with the children? Baby will almost have forgotten me by the time I come back."

"No, he won't; he'll know you in a moment, and give you his biggest hug. It's no use crying, Patty; young birds must leave the nest some time, and learn to fly for themselves. We shall miss you as much as you miss us, but we must brace our minds to bear it, because it's one of those partings that have to come, and are for the best after all. Think what a splendid thing it is for you to be going to such a school as Morton Priory! I only wish I had had such advantages when I was a girl. You must work hard, and make the very most of your time there."

"I'll do my best, but I'm not clever," said Patty, "and I'm afraid I never shall be. Mother, dearest, you're actually crying too! What a horrid, selfish, nasty wretch I am! I believe it's just as bad for you as it is for me. There! I'm not going to say another word, and if I do, please give me a smack. I'm ever so ashamed to have made my darling little Mother cry!"

She got off the bed, and giving a hard scrub to her eyes, stuffed her handkerchief back into her pocket with a determined air, as if the tears went with it. All the same, her voice sounded choky, and there were such bright drops glistening on Mrs. Hirst's eyelashes, that I think they both felt it a welcome interruption when a loud tramping was suddenly heard on the stairs, and four children burst tumultuously into the room: a girl of eleven, two boys of nine and seven, and a younger girl of about five years old.

"We ran all the way home from school," they cried. "We didn't wait a single minute to talk to anybody. Oh! have you packed Patty's box already? We did so want to watch you do it!"

"Go to the nursery, children," said Mrs. Hirst, "I cannot have your meddlesome little fingers here. Robin, put down that hat immediately! Wilfred, you're not to open that bag! No, Kitty, my pet, you mustn't peep inside parcels. Milly, take them away, and make them wash their hands. I didn't expect you all home so soon."

"I'll go with them, Mother," said Patty, taking the noisy four under her elder sisterly wing, and escorting them to their own domain, where Mary, the nurse, was endeavouring to attend to the baby, while at the same time she restrained three-year-old Rowley from making acquaintance with the interior of the coal box. "Did you give Miss Dawson my message, Milly? You forgot? Oh, what a careless girl you are! I shall have to write her a letter. No, it's no use your running back now. There wouldn't be time before tea, it's almost ready."

Patty helped the children to put on pinafores and tidy their hair, washed Rowley's hands, and seated him in his high chair at the table, then made herself so useful in passing bread and butter, spreading jam, and handing round mugs of milk, that Mary gave a heartfelt sigh of regret.

"I simply don't know what we'll do without you when you've gone, Miss Patty," she said dolefully.

"Oh! I wish I were going too!" cried Milly. "What lovely fun it would be! Imagine having a gymnasium, and climbing poles, and walking on planks. Muriel told me all about it when she was over here. She said she learnt to swarm up a rope like sailors do. And there's a swimming bath, and hockey, and cricket, and tennis. You can't think how I envy you, Patty. You're the luckiest girl in the world. It will seem so slow to stay on at Miss Dawson's. I shan't like it one scrap now."

"Will they toss you in a blanket, Patty," enquired Robin eagerly, "like they did Cousin Horace when first he went to school, or twist your arm round and punch it?"

"Of course not," replied Patty, laughing; "those things are only done in boys' schools. Girls don't play such silly tricks; they don't 'punch' people at all."

"They do sometimes," declared Robin; "Milly gave me a horrid——"

"Be quiet!" said Milly quickly, administering what appeared to be a kick under the table. "You deserved anything you got, and if you say a word more I'll tell about—you know what!"

"If you dare!"

"Be quiet, then."

"I will now, but wait till I catch you afterwards!" and Robin, throwing her an indignant glance, applied himself so diligently to his bread and butter, that he had no opportunity for further remarks; while Patty, wisely ignoring the quarrel, turned the conversation back to the safer channel of her future experiences, which at present seemed the most absorbing topic they could have to discuss.

"There'll be a great many more girls there than at Miss Dawson's," she began.

"How many?" asked Milly.

"I believe there are about seventy, and at least half of them will be older than I am. Muriel says some of the top class have turned eighteen, and wear their hair up. I shall only be one of the younger ones."

"How funny!" giggled the children. "Will they give you easy lessons, then?"

"Compound addition and the first declension?" suggested Robin.

"Or spelling and tables?" said Wilfred.

"Will Patty do pot-hooks and learning to read, like me?" said Kitty.

"You will find it easier, though, if you're one of the youngest, won't you?" said Milly.

"No, indeed. I expect all the work will be much harder than anything I've ever done yet. It won't be all hockey and gymnasium, I can tell you. I'm afraid I shall find I'm behind most of the other girls."

"Oh, Patty, and you were always top at Miss Dawson's!"

"That's quite different. It's easy enough to be top when there are only four girls in a class, and two of them as stupid as the Simpsons. I may very likely turn out bottom at The Priory."

"You won't! You won't!" cried Milly. "I heard Miss Dawson tell Mother you were one of her best workers, and she knew you'd do well wherever you went. There, you needn't blush! It wasn't anything very particular, after all. If she'd been talking about me, I'd far rather she'd said I was a good runner, and could catch a ball without missing it every time it was thrown to me."

"She did say something about you, though: I heard her," volunteered Robin.

"Then you shouldn't have listened, and you've no need to tell. I hate tell-tales!" said Milly, forestalling his offered confidence. "If you've finished tea, you'd better go and feed the guinea-pigs. Patty, do come and help me to trace my map, it's the last evening but one that you'll be here; and I want you to show me how to do G.C.M., because I was looking out of the window this morning when Miss Dawson told us, and I can't work any of my sums until I know. Come into the summer-house, where we can get a little peace and quiet;" and hastily swallowing her last fragment of bread and butter, she caught up her school satchel, and beckoning persuasively to her sister, led the way downstairs, and out into the garden.

CHAPTER II

The Priory

As this story mostly concerns Patty, I should like to describe her exactly as she looked when she made her first start into that new, strange world where everything was going to be so different from the quiet home where she had spent the thirteen years of her life. She was not very tall nor very short, just an ordinary, healthy, well-grown girl, with a round, rather childish face, plump rosy cheeks, a nose that had not yet decided what shape it meant to be, a mouth that for beauty might certainly have been smaller, a frank pair of blue eyes, and hair that had been flaxen when she was younger, but now, to her mother's regret, was fast turning as brown as it could. No one could really call Patty pretty, but she had such a merry, pleasant, sunny, smiling look about her, that she always somehow made people feel like smiling too, and put them into a good temper in spite of themselves. She was neither dull nor particularly clever, only possessed of average abilities, able to remember lessons when she tried hard, and gifted with a certain capacity for plodding, but not in the least brilliant over anything she undertook. She was never likely to win fame, or set the Thames on fire, but she was one of those cosy, thoughtful, cheery, lovable home girls, who are often a great deal more pleasant to live with than some who have greater talents; and she had a magic way of making things go smoothly in the household, and dropping oil on all the little creaking hinges of life, without anybody quite discovering how it was done. Patty's father was a busy doctor in the small country town of Kirkstone. He was out nearly the whole day long, driving about in his high gig to visit people in distant farms and villages, and had very little time to give to his own family, so they were obliged to make the most of the few delightful half-hours he could manage to spare for them now and then. Patty, as his eldest daughter, held a special place in his heart. She was already quite a nice companion for him, and I think there was no greater treat for both than on those occasions when she was able to tuck herself into the gig by his side, ready to open gates, and hold the reins while he paid his visits. Patty loved those long drives along the quiet roads. She did not care whether the weather were wet or fine, hot or cold. It did not matter in the least if it snowed or hailed, provided her father was there to talk to, and they could indulge in those confidential chats that seemed to bring them so near together, and made her feel quite a little woman instead of only a girl of thirteen. It was not often, however, that Patty could be absent for the many hours of a doctor's country round. School and lessons claimed most of her time, and even on Saturdays she was so useful at home that they found it difficult to manage without her. Seven younger brothers and sisters all looked to Patty to settle their quarrels, hem their boat sails, dress their dolls, kiss their bumps and bruises better, sympathize with their small woes and troubles, tell them stories, invent new games, and generally take the lead in all the important matters of the nursery. She was her mother's right hand, and from the time she was old enough to feel herself a little older than the rest, she had helped to stitch on buttons, wash chubby faces, fasten tiny shoes, comb curly heads, keep small fingers out of mischief and small limbs from danger, and support the cause of law and order by an emphatic "don't" or "mustn't" when necessary. Patty often congratulated herself on the fact that she had taught five babies to walk. She was very proud of the family, beginning with Basil, who was only a year younger than herself, though not nearly so capable and reliable, and ending with the fat baby who had not yet found his feet, while in between came harum-scarum Milly, boisterous Robin and Wilfred, coaxing, bewitching little Kitty, and round-faced, stolid, three-year-old Rowland, whose name was generally corrupted to Roly-Poly, because it seemed so exactly to suit him.

It had never occurred to Patty that life could ever be very much different from what she was accustomed to. She had seldom been away from Kirkstone, only for short visits to relations or a seaside holiday, and all her horizon was bounded by her home. She went to a day school, where she was one of the elder girls, and felt obliged, even in the midst of her lessons, to keep an eye on Milly's behaviour, and to consider herself responsible for the good conduct of Robin, Wilfred, and Kitty, who were also Miss Dawson's pupils. It was quite anxious work for her to get them off in time in the mornings; to ensure that they did not leave their books at home, or forget their macintoshes on showery days, or lose their slates and pencils; to help to lace their boots, and put on their hats neatly; to make Milly and Kitty wear their gloves, and prevent Robin and Wilfred from filling their pockets with nut shells, stones, frogs, or other unsuitable articles which were apt to stray out in class and call down the vials of the mistress's wrath upon their heads. She saw that they learnt their home lessons, did their sums, practised their due portions upon the piano: and it took up so much of her own time, that she had to work hard to get in even the moderate amount of preparation that was deemed necessary at Miss Dawson's. It had meant a very great change, therefore, when her uncle had written offering to send Patty to Morton Priory with her cousin Muriel. It would have been quite impossible for Dr. Hirst, burdened as he was with a large family and a not too ample income, to place any of his children at expensive boarding schools. Basil, indeed, went by train daily to Winborough, ten miles off, where there was an excellent boys' college; but no better teaching than Miss Dawson could give seemed in store for Patty, until this sudden good fortune had been thrust upon her. Mr. Pearson, her uncle, was a wealthy man, who had only one daughter. It had occurred to him that it would be nice for the two girls to spend their schooldays together, and he had generously undertaken the full charges of his niece's education, declaring she should have exactly the same advantages as her cousin. He had been fond of his sister in their childhood, and thought how suitable it seemed for Muriel, who was three months younger than Patty, to have the latter for a companion during the years he wished her to remain at The Priory.

"Patty is such a good, conscientious child," he wrote to Mrs. Hirst, "I know she will look after her cousin, and stand by her in any trouble. I can trust her to be a true and loyal friend, and it will be a comfort to me to think that Muriel has anyone so stanch and steady on whom to depend. If Patty will consider my girl her special charge while she is at The Priory, she will amply repay me for anything I may expend on her behalf. It is a bargain to which I am sure she will agree, and which I feel certain she will be ready to keep."

Such a tremendous occasion as being sent away to school naturally marked an epoch in Patty's life, though she looked upon the event with mixed feelings. Sometimes it seemed terrible to her to have to leave her dear ones at home, and she shrank from the parting with an almost morbid fear lest she should never see them all again; then a more sensible mood would prevail, and she would be so glad to think she was going, and so excited about it, that she could scarcely wait until the summer holidays were over, and the autumn term should begin. The one thing which troubled her most was the charge which had been laid upon her to look after her cousin. The latter was such a totally different girl from herself, that unfortunately she felt they had little in common; and though she was anxious to do her utmost to prove the stanch friend in need that her uncle required, she was sure that Muriel would greatly resent all interference, and she did not anticipate an easy task. She did not like to discuss the question much with her father and mother. They seemed so pained at the thought that the two girls should not agree, and so wishful that their schooldays should bring them nearer together, that she determined not to mention the subject again, and could only hope that her fears might not be fulfilled. What the future held in store for her, and what experiences she was to encounter in her new life at Morton Priory, it is the object of this story to relate.

A neatly printed notice had been forwarded to Dr. Hirst, reminding him that the autumn term reopened on September 20th, and that it was requested that all pupils should return on that day, arriving not later than five o'clock in the afternoon. Patty wondered how anybody could be in danger of forgetting such an important date, and from counting the days had come to counting the hours and even the minutes up to that particular moment when she must set out on her travels. To her great delight, her father and mother had decided to take a little holiday and escort her safely to school. They were anxious to see The Priory for themselves, and to make the acquaintance of Miss Lincoln, the headmistress, with whom they had already held some correspondence; and they both felt they would be much better satisfied if they could picture Patty in her new surroundings, and leave her looking tolerably cheerful and happy there. After a terrible parting from the children, Patty tore herself away at last from their hugs and kisses, and sat blinking back tears until the cab reached the station, in spite of Dr. Hirst's efforts to distract her attention. She brightened up, however, in the train. It seemed so important to be sitting there with a new brown leather bag in the rack over her head, and a new box in the luggage van, both marked with her own initials, and to feel she was bound for such a particularly interesting destination. It was a rather tedious cross-country journey. After they had changed twice, and found themselves on the main line at a busy junction, the long corridor carriage was suddenly filled up with so many girls of various ages, that Patty began to think she must be face to face with some of her school-fellows, who no doubt were arriving by the same train as herself. Two mistresses, who were waiting on the platform, marshalled the excited, chattering young people to their places, and saw to the safe bestowal of their luggage—evidently no light task, for there were many outcries after bags and parcels of wraps and umbrellas, forgotten in the bustle of changing, and porters were sent hurrying hither and thither to recover the lost property. Everybody was at length on board the train, including three girls who made a great sensation at the last moment by racing down the platform to get chocolates from the automatic machine, and were nearly left behind, to the equal indignation of the guard and the two teachers. The Hirsts' compartment was crammed as tightly as it could be: five girls managed to screw themselves into the space of four, and one, who could find no seat at all, sat in turns on the others' knees. Two amongst them at once attracted Patty's notice. One, a fair-haired girl of about the same age as herself, cried persistently and unrestrainedly, burying her face in the window curtain, and refusing all comfort, though her companions pressed chocolates, caramels, mint rock, jujubes, and walnut toffee upon her with well-meant sympathy.

"Oh, do stop, Avis! You make the place quite damp. No one would think it was your fourth term. I hope you've brought a macintosh pillow, if you're going to turn on the waterworks like this. Wipe your eyes, and have a peppermint cream. I always take them when I feel homesick. There's nothing does one so much good."

The speaker was a merry, bonny-looking girl of perhaps fifteen, with bright brown eyes, a clear complexion, a freckled nose, very white teeth, and curly brown hair tied with a red ribbon. Patty thought she must surely have spent all her pocket money at the confectioner's before she came away —such endless packets of sweets came out of the Gladstone bag which she held on her knee, and disappeared with such startling rapidity that Dr. Hirst looked on in horror.

"I got hold of my eldest brother," she explained to a companion. "I told him I shouldn't be allowed a solitary chocolate drop at The Priory, and how I should be simply yearning even for treacle toffee. He laughed, and said I should have a good time before I got there, at any rate, so we went into town, and he bought me absolutely anything I wanted. Have another caramel, Winnie? It's no use keeping them. Miss Rowe'll confiscate them all if she finds them in my bag. You won't have the chance of any more sweets for thirteen weeks, remember!"

"Not unless she can manage to get up a cough," said a girl whom the others addressed as Ida, "and it depends whether you like Miss Lincoln's cough drops or not. I think they're hateful myself, and taste like medicine, but Dorothy Dawson loves them. She made her throat quite sore one day last term with trying to cough all through the history class, and Miss Lincoln didn't give her any after all. She only told her to go and take a glass of water. Dolly was so disgusted! No, thanks, Enid! I really can't manage another. There are limits, you know, even for me."

"But we simply must finish them up."

"Then finish them yourself."

"She'll be ill if she does," said the short, rosy-faced girl called Winnie. "I don't believe you've stopped eating sweets, Enid, since you got into the train. You'll have a horrible headache to-morrow, see if you don't!"

"I'll call it homesickness if I do," laughed Enid, "and then everybody will sympathize with me. Look here, Avis, if you insist on crying over the window curtains you'll take the colour out of them, and the company will bring an action for damages. They're so dusty, too. Your face is all in streaks of black. Let me rub it off for you. Winnie, lend me your bottle of eau de Cologne, that's a dear. I have a clean handkerchief here. That's better. Now do cheer up, and put your hat straight; we shall be there in about five minutes."

Patty sat surveying these new girl comrades with deep interest. Avis and Enid particularly claimed her attention. She had a kindred feeling for the grief of the one, and the lively manner and bright chat of the other were attractive, while a look in the merry brown eyes, when they happened to glance her way, made her think their owner would be willing to make friends. There was no opportunity, however, to speak, and the train having reached Morton, everyone turned out in a hurry. In the bustle of collecting handbags and umbrellas and identifying her own box from the huge pile of similar luggage on the platform, she lost sight of her fellow-travellers, and only thought she noticed Enid's blue dress disappearing inside a station omnibus, and Winnie's black hat whisk past her in a closely packed landau.

"Muriel was to arrive by the earlier train," said Dr. Hirst, as he put Patty's belongings into a cab. "No doubt we shall find her waiting for us at The Priory. What a number of girls! And everyone seems to have brought a hockey stick. We shall have to ask Miss Lincoln to get one for you, Patty. If the pretty, dark girl who was in our compartment isn't ill to-morrow, I shall be much surprised. I'm sure she deserves to be. If I were her medical man, I should order her a dose of rhubarb and sal volatile. She's going to call it homesickness, the young rascal, is she? She looks as if she could be ready to play pranks. If they would consult me, I'd soon find a cure!" And the doctor chuckled with amusement at the idea.

The Priory was about a mile away from the railway station, and it was with a beating heart and a queer lump in her throat that Patty found herself stepping from the cab and alighting at a great doorway ornamented with ecclesiastical carvings, and, giving a hasty glance round a courtyard where girls of various ages seemed already to be collected, realized that she had at length reached school. In the fourteenth century Morton Priory had been a monastery of the Franciscan order, and it now seemed a strange irony of fate that feminine petticoats should reign supreme within the very walls where the grey brothers had lived in such seclusion. The old refectory where they had dined, and the cloister where they had been wont to meditate, were now given up to a lively, laughing crew of girls, whose serge skirts and white blouses among the quaint surroundings made a curious blending of ancient and modern. What remained of the monastic building occupied one side of a large quadrangle, while the other three sides were taken up with modern additions, erected, however, in such excellent taste, and so closely in accordance with the architecture of the older portion, that the whole had a strictly mediæval appearance. In the centre of the courtyard was a pretty Italian garden, with neat box edgings, where stood the sundial which had marked the hours for the monks who once paced there, and still remained an old-world protest against the big clock in the tower over the gymnasium that set the time for the clanging school bell. Situated in the midst of beautiful scenery, the large grounds formed a little self-contained kingdom, shut off from the rest of the world: the numerous tennis courts and the playing fields provided ample space for outdoor sports; the home farm supplied milk, butter, and eggs; the kitchen garden grew the fruit and vegetables; while a small sanatorium in a breezy corner ensured a safe retreat for anyone who happened to be placed upon the sick list.

Parents were received in the library by Miss Lincoln, who spoke a few pleasant words to Dr. and Mrs. Hirst about Patty's education and attainments, and then, as other visitors arrived, passed them on to an under-mistress, who took them to have tea in the drawing-room, and afterwards showed them round the school. To Patty, fresh from Miss Dawson's modest arrangements, it seemed indeed a new world, and she looked with eager eyes at the classrooms with their Girton desks, their maps and their blackboards, the studio with its array of casts, models, and easels, the row of little practising rooms, each with piano, music stool, and a chair for the teacher; and she gazed almost with awe at the laboratory with its mysterious bottles and retorts, and the gymnasium fitted with ropes, bars, and other appliances as yet unknown to her. Her bag was already placed on the chair in her neat cubicle, though her box had not been carried upstairs, and her mother was able to note with approval the excellent arrangements of the bedroom, curtained off as it was into four parts.

"I'm sorry you will not be with your cousin," said Mrs. Hirst, "but no doubt you'll soon get to know your room mates. I should like to see Muriel before we go. I wonder where she is! We must be quick, as we have only ten minutes left before we must start again to the station."

Miss Graveson, the mistress, volunteered to send in search of her, and a girl started on an urgent hunt through the school; but evidently it was a difficult task, for it was only when the Hirsts' cab was at the door that she returned with the object of her quest.

Muriel was a remarkably pretty girl, slight and graceful, with eyes as blue as forget-me-nots, and long, silky, golden hair; she was generally very artistically dressed, and always looked like a picture, a fact of which she was extremely well aware. She greeted her uncle and aunt without much enthusiasm, gave Patty her cheek to kiss, and did not seem particularly delighted at having been called to speak to them.

"I expected we should have seen you before, dear," said Mrs. Hirst. "I felt quite unhappy at the idea of leaving Patty alone, but now you are here to show her the ways of The Priory, I'm sure she'll be all right. Muriel will be able to tell you everything, Patty, so I give you into her hands. Now good-bye, my darling child! Don't fret, and write to us as soon as you can. We shall be looking forward to your first letter, and please let it be a cheerful one."

CHAPTER III

First Impressions

Patty certainly felt anything but cheerful as she stood at the top of the steps to watch her father and mother drive away, though she put on a brave face, and waved a vigorous farewell.

"They've only just time to catch their train," she said, turning to Muriel. "I hope the man will go fast. It would be so tiresome for them to miss it."

"Why aren't they staying all night at the Queen's Hotel?" asked Muriel. "Father and Mother always do when they come to see me and so do most of the girls' friends."

"Father wouldn't be able to spare the time," said Patty, thinking privately that the expense would also be a consideration, though she did not say that aloud. "He must get home to look after his patients, you know. Mr. Barnes, our new assistant, isn't very clever, and several people are seriously ill, and can't be left long."

Muriel shrugged her shoulders.

"I wouldn't mention they'd brought you, then," she replied. "It's considered the correct thing for one's parents to stay at the Queen's, and the girls will think it so queer if yours haven't. What bedroom are you in?"

"No. 7. I hope it's a nice one?"

"Oh, tolerable! Not so nice as mine. I'm in No. 16, on the other landing, with three of my best friends."

"Do you know who's in my room?"

"Nobody at all particular; only May Firth, Ella Johnson, and Doris Kennedy. Do you see that new girl crossing the quad? I believe she comes from our part of the world. She was starting too when I was setting off; they nearly put her in my carriage, only luckily the guard had locked the door."

"What's her name? I don't remember seeing her at Waverton."

"I daresay not. Her name's Jean Bannerman, and she lives in one of those houses at the end of the park. I met her once at a party, but we don't know them at all."

"Does she seem nice?"

"I'm sure I can't tell. I wasn't much impressed with her. Have you unpacked?"

"No, not yet. My box hasn't been brought upstairs."

"It's there now. I saw John carrying it to your room. I should think you'd better go and take your things out."

"Won't you come with me, Muriel?" asked Patty, rather shyly. "I don't know where I'm expected to put my clothes."

"Haven't time," said Muriel, shaking her head. "I've got all my own to do. It's easy enough; you've only to pop them into your drawers and your wardrobe. Supper's at seven in the refectory. Why, there's Gwendolen Farmer. I simply must go and speak to her. Ta-ta!"

And Muriel ran away to the other side of the quadrangle, leaving Patty standing alone upon the steps.

Thus suddenly deserted, the latter watched for a moment to see if her cousin meant to come back, but Muriel, after greeting the newcomer with much affection, linked her arm in hers, and without even turning her head to look round, walked through a doorway opposite, and was lost to sight. Patty went upstairs to her cubicle with a rather sore feeling in her heart, against which she made a violent effort to struggle. After all, she argued to herself, it was only natural that Muriel, who must have so many friends in the school, should be so anxious to see them all again after the long summer holidays. She would no doubt be waiting in the refectory to show her to her seat, and would then, perhaps, introduce her to a few special companions.

She could not mean absolutely to ignore her, and it was absurd to take offence needlessly.

"I'm her own relation, and she surely can't forget that," thought Patty. "She's busy now, but she'll be nicer to me later on."

Each bedroom at The Priory was divided into four cubicles by means of curtains hung on brass rods, and each cubicle contained its own little bed, chest of drawers, washstand, and small wardrobe. Patty was lucky enough to have a window that looked out over the playing fields, otherwise her division was exactly the same as the rest. The three other occupants appeared to have already unpacked: their nightdress cases were laid on their beds, their sponges on their washstands, various photo frames, books, and ornaments adorned their dressing-tables, and their curtains were drawn back, as was the rule when the cubicles were not occupied, to allow a free current of air through the room. Patty unlocked her box, and set to work to arrange her various possessions, placing the photo of the family group, which had been a parting present from home, in a prominent position, and trying to stifle the longing to see all the dear, familiar faces again. The nightdress case, which she had thought so beautiful when she was packing, looked quite plain and ordinary by the side of the three elaborately worked ones on the other beds. She had certainly nothing so dainty as the pale-pink, quilted silk dressing-gown that she could see hanging on a peg behind the door, nor did she possess cut-glass scent bottles, such as stood on the dressing-table in the cubicle opposite; nevertheless Patty put her things away with a certain pride of ownership, and when all was neatly finished, glanced round her new quarters with much satisfaction. It was scarcely six o'clock, and supper was not until seven, so she decided to go downstairs again on the chance of finding Muriel, who by this time must surely have finished her own unpacking. She waited in the hall for a few minutes, not quite knowing what to do, until a mistress, hurrying by, noticed her standing there, and directed her to the recreation room. Here a number of girls appeared to be collected: a pair of bosom friends occupied one window, and five pigtails in close proximity took up another; by the empty fire grate a group of four stood talking photography with a short fat girl in spectacles, seated on the edge of the table; while others were continually passing in and out to announce their own arrival, or to search for absent companions. Several glanced at Patty, but nobody spoke to her, or paid any particular attention, so she walked over to the sofa, and taking a book which she found there, sat idly turning the pages without reading them, and feeling very uncomfortable and extremely homesick. Everybody in the room, she thought, seemed talking, laughing, and joking with everyone else, and she was the only stranger amongst them. No, she was mistaken. There was one girl as solitary as herself, sitting on the music stool, and turning over a pile of old pieces and songs that lay on the top of the piano. She was an interesting-looking girl, with good features, grey eyes with very long dark lashes, a clear pale complexion, as creamy as if it had been bathed in milk, and light-brown hair that curled charmingly round her forehead. She did not appear to find her occupation very absorbing, for she glanced every now and then in Patty's direction, and finally, putting the music back on the piano, came quietly across the room and sat down beside her on the sofa.

"I suppose you're new, aren't you?" she said. "So am I. We seem rather out of it at present, don't we? Do you know any of these girls?"

"No," replied Patty, "not one of them. I've only just come a little while ago."

"Yes, I saw your cab drive up. I arrived by the earlier train, so I've had more time to get used to it. I can't say I like it at all yet, though. To tell you the truth, I don't mind confessing I'd give everything in the world to find myself at home again."

This was so exactly Patty's present state of mind, that she felt it established a bond of sympathy at once with her companion, and encouraged her sufficiently to enquire her name.

"Jean Bannerman," said the girl, "and I'm almost fifteen. What's yours?"

"Patty Hirst, and I shall be fourteen in October."

"Then I'm nearly a year older than you, for my birthday's in November. Which bedroom are you in?"

"No. 7."

"I'm in No. 10. I don't know what my room mates are like yet. I hope they're nice. I wish you had been one of them. It seems so horrid when everything and everybody are strange. Isn't it dreadfully noisy here? Suppose we go into the courtyard for a little while. It's quite light yet, and I see ever so many girls out there. Do you know your way about the school?"

"Yes—no—yes," replied Patty, hesitatingly.

"Which do you mean?" asked Jean, smiling.

"I mean 'yes'," said Patty. "A teacher showed us round, but I'm afraid I didn't take very much notice, because, you see, Father and Mother were just leaving, and I——"

Jean gave a nod of comprehension.

"Then we'll go and explore," she said. "There don't seem to be any particular rules nor any preparation the first evening. Everybody is unpacking, and I think we may do as we like until supper. Come along!"

Nothing loth, Patty rose and joined her companion. She was anxious to see something of the new life into which she had been launched, and she looked with curiosity round the large quadrangle, which appeared at present to be the central heart of the school. Here girls of ages varying from thirteen to eighteen were assembled, comparing holiday experiences, examining each other's tennis rackets or hockey sticks, passing jokes, or eagerly enquiring for news on various class topics. To Patty it seemed almost bewildering to see so many school-fellows, and she wondered whether it would ever become possible to learn to distinguish their various faces, and to call each one by her right name.

"I suppose we shall get to know them in time," she said, "but it will be confusing at first. Do you notice that some of the big girls wear badges? I wonder what that means?"

"Let us ask somebody," said Jean, glancing round to see if there were anyone near to whom she might venture to address her enquiry. "That fair girl sitting on the bench over there looks nice; I'm sure she would tell us. I don't think she's new, because she was talking to some of the others a minute ago."

Patty turned in the direction indicated, and recognized the fellow-traveller who had wept so copiously in the train, and whom her companions had called Avis. Her tears were dried, but she still appeared pensive. She held a blotter on her knee, and with a fountain pen was evidently already beginning a letter home. She put it aside when Jean spoke to her, and answered pleasantly:

"Of course I can tell you. The badges are worn by the prefects. They're the six top girls, and they're supposed to keep order. It's a tremendous honour to be a prefect. Phyllis Chambers is head of the school this year. We're all glad, because she's so jolly, and she was our tennis champion last summer. There she is!—that girl in the grey dress. She won us four matches against other schools. We were so proud of her."

"Isn't she champion now?"

"We don't play tennis this term; it's all hockey. I think Mabel Morgan is better at that. You'll both be in the lower school team, of course. Do you know what classes you're in?"

"Not yet," said Patty. "There's to be an exam. to-morrow morning. I'm afraid I shan't be very high up."

"Oh, you may do better than you expect. Exams. are such a chance. It's just whether you happen to get a nice set of questions or not. I wonder if you'll be in my class. I'm in the upper fourth, Miss Harper's."

"Is she nice?"

"Well, some adore her, and some don't care for her at all. It depends a good deal on yourself. She likes the ones who work, but she can be dreadfully sarcastic if she thinks you're stupid or lazy. She's fearfully clever, and says such witty things sometimes. Half-a-dozen of the girls absolutely worship her, but she's very fair, and won't have favourites. I like her better than Miss Rowe."

"Who is she?"

"The second mistress in our class. You see, the fourth is in two divisions, an upper and a lower; we do a few lessons together and some separately.

Miss Harper takes history and literature, and what I call the more interesting things, and Miss Rowe takes arithmetic and analysis, and looks after our preparation. There are twenty girls altogether, counting both divisions. It's the largest class in the school. There are only ten in the fifth."

"Which is the nicest teacher of all?" asked Jean.

"I think most of us like Miss Latimer best, the games mistress. She's very popular with everybody. You see, we always have such fun at gymnastics, and of course we love hockey and cricket. She teaches us swimming too, but that's only during the summer term. There's the bell! We must go in to supper. Do you know your way to the refectory? We all settle places on the first evening, so it's rather exciting. Perhaps you'd like to come with me?"

Patty would have replied in the affirmative, but at that moment she happened to notice Muriel crossing the quadrangle, as she thought, in search of her, and saying she had better wait, she allowed Jean and Avis to go indoors without her. She was perfectly certain that Muriel must have seen her, but, greatly to her surprise, her cousin turned aside and claimed acquaintance with a chestnut-haired girl, with whom she hastened into the house without bestowing a look in Patty's direction. The great clanging bell was still ringing in the tower over the gymnasium, and groups of girls came hurrying towards the refectory from all parts of the building.

"Be quick, my dear," said a teacher, passing Patty, and noticing her hesitation. "Everyone is going to supper. Come with me, and I will find a place for you."

Patty followed, rather nervous, but thankful that somebody would show her where she must sit. The refectory was almost full when they entered. It was a large room, with a groined roof like a church, and stained-glass windows at either side. A long table occupied the entire length, and at one end was a raised dais, with another table for the mistresses. It resembled in this respect the hall of a college, and was a subject of great pride to Miss Lincoln, who liked to think that the school had its meals in the same place where the old monks had dined six hundred years ago. Muriel was seated towards the centre of the table, chatting to several friends in whose company she seemed entirely absorbed. There was evidently no room in her vicinity, and the teacher moved farther along and found a place for Patty nearer the end. She was between two girls rather older than herself, neither of whom spoke to her. One appeared to be in an uncommunicative frame of mind, and answered abruptly when a neighbour asked her a question, and the other was occupied with a conversation with two schoolmates at the opposite side of the table. Patty ate her supper, therefore, in silence, feeling exceedingly shy, and very much hurt that her cousin should have treated her so unkindly. On her first evening common politeness would have suggested that Muriel might have sought her out and introduced her to a few other girls, instead of leaving her thus friendless and forlorn. Even Jean and Avis were too far away to speak to, and she was yet an absolute outsider to everyone else. There is nothing more solitary than to feel oneself alone in a crowd, and the tears rose to poor Patty's eyes at the remembrance of the nursery at home, where the little ones would just have gone to bed, and Milly and Robin would be learning their lessons for the next day.

When the meal was over, the whole school adjourned to the lecture-room to listen to an opening speech from Miss Lincoln, who usually began the term with an address to her pupils. The singing class sang a few glees, and there was a recitation by one of the prefects; after that came prayers, and then it was bedtime. Patty was escorted to No. 7 by the same teacher who had taken her to the refectory, and who, she learnt, was Miss Rowe, the second mistress of the fourth class. The curtains of the other cubicles were closely drawn, so she did not catch a glimpse of her companions, and as all conversation was strictly forbidden, the room was in silence. Patty went to bed in the very lowest of spirits. It had not seemed a favourable beginning to her school life, and unless things improved a little she was sure she could never be happy.

"I suppose I must try and make the best of it," she thought; "and one thing I'm determined about, however wretched I feel, I'm not going to write miserable letters home and upset Mother. She wanted me so much to like The Priory, so I won't let her know, even if nobody ever does talk to me or be nice. There are eighty-nine days before I can go back, and this is one off, at any rate. I expect they'll go by somehow, though I wish I could skip them all, and this were the last day of the term instead of only the first."

CHAPTER IV

A Maiden all Forlorn

PATTY awoke next morning with a vague, drowsy, comfortable impression that she was in her own room at home, with Milly in the other bed, and she was just going to turn over and fall happily asleep again, when she suddenly remembered where she was, and felt as if her heart, instead of being light and cheerful as usual, had changed into lead or some substance of an equally weighty description. She realized that it was the sound of voices that had disturbed her. Two girls in the opposite cubicles were talking together, in low tones, certainly, but loud enough to be most distinctly audible.

"It is a shame, Doris," said the first, "when you and I and Beatrice and May had all put our names down for a bedroom together, and Miss Graveson had almost promised we should have this one! And she won't say why not, either, only that Miss Lincoln had arranged it this way."

"It's perfectly disgusting," replied the other. "Miss Lincoln's absolutely mean. And Beatrice is as disappointed about it as we are. She's in No. 12, with Ada and Carrie Hardman. Think of having to share your room with the Hardmans! Beatrice says she doesn't intend even to speak to them."

"It's just as bad for us. We don't want this new girl. Why couldn't Miss Lincoln put her with the Hardmans, and let Beatrice come to No. 7?"

"Oh, I don't know, except that she knew we were so anxious about it. We shan't have any fun now. I expect she'll be dreadfully priggish and proper."

"Have you seen her?"

"Only for a moment. Ida Haslam pointed her out to me in the recreation room. I thought she seemed rather prim. At any rate, she doesn't look nearly as nice as Beatrice."

"She certainly couldn't be that."

"I wish she hadn't come, and I vote we don't make any fuss over her."

"I'm not going to, I assure you!"

"Well, I shan't either. She can take care of herself, and make friends with anybody she likes. Only it's a horrible nuisance to be obliged to have her in our room. Look here, Ella, suppose we——"

But here it suddenly dawned upon Patty that she was listening to what was not intended for her ears, so she gave such a very wide-awake cough that the speaker stopped, and after a suppressed giggle, apparently drew aside the curtain of her cubicle, leaned out of bed, and continued her remarks in a subdued whisper. It certainly was not particularly encouraging for Patty to find she was so unwelcome in No. 7. It seemed too bad that her room mates should be prejudiced against her before they had really made her acquaintance. It was not her fault that she had been put in the place of the companion they preferred, and it was unfair and unkind to have a grudge against her on that account. She wondered if Jean Bannerman would be accorded as cold a reception in No. 10. Jean, at any rate, had seemed friendly, and their little walk round the quadrangle had been so far the only bright spot since her arrival. She had not much time, however, for further reflections; a loud bell in the passage gave the signal for rising, and, afraid of being late, she got up at once. Judging from the sounds in the other cubicles, Doris and Ella appeared to have some difficulty in waking May, who was evidently a heavy sleeper, and all three indulged in many yawns and groans before they finally tore themselves out of bed, and hurried rapidly through their toilets, chatting meanwhile about various affairs which were quite unintelligible to anyone who had not yet learnt to take part in the life at The Priory.

Patty was able to say good morning to Jean, and to sit next to her at prayers, but they were obliged to separate in the refectory, and breakfast was as silent a meal as supper of the night before. Lessons began at nine o'clock, and Patty found herself escorted by Miss Rowe to a small empty classroom, where she was to undergo an entrance examination. All the other new girls, including Jean, had already taken this examination at home, the papers having been sent to them by post; but owing to a mistake, this preliminary had been omitted in Patty's case, and she must now give some proof of her attainments before she could be placed in any form. It was an anxious morning for her. She wrote on steadily, but it was difficult to do herself justice, as the history paper was on a period she had not studied specially, and the geography also covered new ground. She was allowed an hour for each, and gave a sigh of relief when the clock at last struck eleven, and Miss Rowe took her to the pantry for lunch. This was a very informal affair; the girls ran in as they liked, and helped themselves to glasses of milk and slices of thick bread and butter, which were placed in readiness for them. Patty looked eagerly among the chattering throng for any face that she knew, but though girls were hurrying in and out the whole time she was there, she saw neither Jean, Avis, nor Muriel. All seemed occupied in discussing school topics, and far too busy to notice her, and when the great bell rang, everyone fled hastily to lecture or classroom, and left her still standing with her empty glass in her hand. She put it down leisurely, and was just wondering what to do next, when Miss Rowe came bustling up.

"Come along at once, Patty!" she said, in a rather peremptory tone. "Didn't you hear the bell?"

"Yes," replied Patty, wondering what she had done amiss.

"Then why are you not back at your desk in the classroom?"

"I didn't know——" began Patty, but Miss Rowe broke in as if she had not the patience to listen to explanations.

"You will have to learn punctuality here," she said. "Any girl who is late for a class loses an order mark. Now be quick and get on with this arithmetic paper. I can only allow you till twelve o'clock for it, and then you must begin the grammar."

Patty obeyed in silence, feeling much subdued. It was rather hard, she thought, that when she was still so new and strange she must be scolded for not keeping the rules of the school. She had not really known that she was expected to hasten back to her examination at the sound of the bell, and had, in fact, been waiting for Miss Rowe to come and fetch her. The latter seemed annoyed. She hurried Patty to her place, and handed her a fresh supply of manuscript paper with very scant ceremony, then, taking up a book, appeared to be preparing some lesson. Patty remembered how Avis had hinted that Miss Rowe was not popular, and she thought she began to understand why. In spite of the urgent necessity of getting on quickly with her sums, she could not help stealing occasional glances at the mistress, whose clear-cut profile, firm mouth, calm grey eyes, and abundant braids of fair hair half attracted and half repelled her. Miss Rowe was barely out of her teens; indeed, it was only a year since she had left school herself to come as assistant governess at The Priory, and she tried to make up for her lack of years by exacting the utmost in the way of discipline, and asserting her dignity upon all occasions. Miss Lincoln, who saw that there was sometimes friction between Miss Rowe and her pupils, interfered as little as she could, thinking the young teacher would soon learn by experience, and it was better to leave her to fight her own battles, and hoping that time and prudence would conquer many difficulties. Patty, of course, did not know all this, but she realized that Miss Rowe was inclined to be impatient and dictatorial, and in consequence began to think that she should not like her. Morning school at The Priory was from nine till one, and the hours from two to four were devoted to outdoor exercise. To-day, however, owing to her examination, Patty was obliged to return after dinner to the classroom, and she was not free until three o'clock, when she handed in her last paper, and was told by Miss Rowe that she might go and join the other girls in the grounds. Very much relieved that her ordeal was over at last, she put on her hat and strolled across the quadrangle under an archway into the garden beyond. She felt tired out and languid. It was a warm September day, and the unwonted exertion of answering so many questions had made her head ache. She wandered aimlessly along the paths, pausing for a few moments at the tennis courts, where a little crowd of spectators stood watching an exciting set, then on towards the playing fields, where more girls appeared to be practising hockey. Everybody seemed to be friends and to be occupied with some game or amusement except herself, and the loneliness of her position struck poor Patty again with full force. Muriel had entirely deserted her, and evidently did not intend to take the slightest notice of her. There had not yet been any opportunity of renewing the acquaintance with either Jean Bannerman or Avis, and nobody else had proffered even a remark.

"EVERYBODY SEEMED TO BE FRIENDS AND TO BE OCCUPIED WITH SOME GAME OR AMUSEMENT EXCEPT HERSELF"

"Do they always boycott new girls like this?" thought Patty. "It was very different at Miss Dawson's. If a fresh girl came we used to be so nice to her, and show her everything. If this is a big school, I'd much rather have a little one. Oh! what can I say to Mother when I write? I can't possibly pretend I'm happy, and I'm sure she'll expect me to mention Muriel. I shall just have to tell her about the exams., and what class I'm in—and I don't even know that myself yet. I must send a letter to-morrow, I promised they should hear by Friday; but I wish I could have told them some better news."

Patty's circumstances were certainly a little exceptional. Miss Lincoln, as a rule, took care that every newcomer was given in charge of some classmate, who was instructed to show her the ways of the school, and make her feel at home there; but knowing that Patty was Muriel's cousin, the headmistress had naturally thought it unnecessary to specially introduce her, expecting she would at once find herself in the midst of a pleasant set of companions. If she had had the slightest suspicion of the true state of the case, she would have been much distressed, as she took great pains to cultivate nice feeling among her girls, and especially to allow no one to be neglected or unkindly treated. Miss Rowe, the only teacher who so far had had anything to do with Patty, had been too busy and occupied to notice whether she appeared to be mixing with the rest of the school, and having dismissed her to the garden, did not give her another thought. Several girls, so Patty learnt afterwards, watched her strolling down the paths, and had half thought of speaking to her: but thinking she was perhaps only looking for some friend, they had not carried out their good intentions, and for the present she was left alone. Tea was at four o'clock, and was followed by preparation until a quarter to seven.

"Miss Lincoln has not yet been able to correct your papers, Patty," said Miss Graveson, "so I cannot set you any definite work; but you can come with me to the Fifth Form room, and I will find something for you to do."

Patty followed obediently to the classroom in question. The ten girls who occupied the desks were all strangers to her, and as strict silence was the rule, there would certainly have been no opportunity for conversation. Everybody seemed working as hard as possible. Some sat with elbows on desks, and their fingers in their ears, evidently committing rules to memory; some were biting their pens in the agonies of composition, and others counting on their fingers as they added up sums. I think Patty will not be blamed very much if she did not pay great attention to the passage which Miss Graveson told her to analyse and parse. She was growing so terribly homesick and dispirited, that she longed to put her head down on the desk and indulge in a good fit of crying, and only her habit of self-control saved her from showing her feelings before her companions. After supper all the members of the lower school were expected to bring their work-bags to the recreation room, and to sit sewing while one of the mistresses read aloud. Patty retired quietly to the sofa, and opening the piece of linen embroidery which she had brought with her, began to stitch in a rather unenthusiastic manner. She felt too shy and dejected to offer any advances to the other girls, and nobody came and sat by her, or made any attempt at friendship. She noticed Muriel enter, and for one second their eyes met, but Muriel deliberately looked the other way, and with heightened colour crossed to the opposite side of the room, cutting her so coolly and decidedly that Patty could not possibly mistake her intention. Jean Bannerman was seated not very far off, talking to Avis, but as their backs were turned to Patty they did not see her, though Jean looked round the room once or twice as if in quest of somebody. I think Patty might perhaps have summoned up sufficient courage to go and speak to them had not Miss Rowe entered, and after an enquiry as to whether all the girls were provided with work, took the armchair which had been reserved for her, and commenced to read aloud. The book was Dickens's *Great Expectations*, and ever afterwards Patty associated the first chapters with an indescribable feeling of misery and wretchedness. Pip's distresses seemed quite in harmony with her state of mind, and she thought she would almost have preferred his adventure with the escaped convict to her own present unhappiness. Troubles always seem at their worst at bedtime, and the memory of home rose up so strongly, that she began to come to the conclusion it would be an absolute impossibility ever to like The Priory in the least. A new difficulty which Patty mastered that evening was the art of crying in bed without making the slightest sound so as to betray her grief to the occupants of the other cubicles—a hard and rather choky achievement, for tears are far more bitter when they must needs be suppressed, and the sorrow that causes them be hidden away.

She rose next day and went to breakfast, feeling still an alien and an outsider. The three girls who shared her bedroom appeared determined to show by their manner how much they resented her presence. They did not even say good morning, though they were passing through the door at exactly the same moment as herself, and they hurried on as fast as they could to avoid walking downstairs with her. In all the large school there seemed nobody to whom she could turn for sympathy or advice. When the first bell rang for lessons, she lingered in the hall wondering where she was expected to go, and was much relieved after a minute or two to see Miss Rowe coming evidently in search of her.

"I've been looking for you, Patty," she said. "You've been placed in the Upper Fourth Form. Come with me at once to the classroom, and I'll show you your desk. Have you brought your pencil box? No; there isn't time to go and fetch it now; you must manage without for this morning. I can lend you this pencil, but be sure you don't forget to return it to me at one o'clock."

The classroom proved large and airy, with four big windows, the lower sashes of which were painted white to prevent wandering eyes straying from lesson books to the view outside. It was fitted with desks arranged to face a low platform on which stood the blackboard, a chair, and a large desk for the teacher. The walls were hung with maps and views of foreign places, and there was a cupboard in the corner, where chalk, new books, ink bottles, and stationery were kept. The vacant desk reserved for Patty proved to be in the middle of the back row, and as she took her seat she looked anxiously to see who were her classmates. All the girls of both the upper and lower divisions were already in their places, and the view of twenty-one dark or fair heads, and twenty-one various coloured hair ribbons was rather bewildering. Muriel was two rows in front, and Jean a little to her left, and in the hasty glance she was able to bestow she noticed Avis and two of the other companions with whom she had travelled to Morton on the day of her arrival. Miss Rowe took the call-over, and entered Patty's name on the register in a neat, firm handwriting; then, mustering the seven members of the lower division, she marched them out of the room for a separate lesson, leaving the platform to Miss Harper, who arrived punctually at the stroke of nine. The mistress of the Fourth Form had a striking personality which could not fail to influence those with whom she came into contact—tall, dark, and handsome, she gave the impression of much strength of will, keen wits, and great abilities. She was a very clever teacher, who liked to push on quick pupils, but was a little ruthless towards stupid girls. She knew how to make the dullest subject entertaining, and expected a high average of work, having no toleration for laziness, and a contempt for incompetence. No girl ever dreamt of whispering or idling during Miss Harper's classes. As a rule, a word or even a look was sufficient to maintain order. She rarely if ever inflicted a punishment for a breach of discipline; to do so, she considered, would be an acknowledgment of her lack of authority, and indeed the girls dreaded one of her scathing reproofs far more than an imposition or the loss of a mark. Her bright, vivacious, interesting style, her fund of appropriate stories for every occasion, and her many amusing remarks and comments, made her extremely popular with her class in spite of her strictness, and the moment she took her place on the platform all eyes were fixed on her clever, intellectual face. The subject of her lecture this morning was the reign of James I, and to Patty, accustomed to Miss Dawson's mild explanations, it was a revelation in the way of teaching. As she had not prepared the chapter, she could, of course, not answer any of the questions asked; but in spite of that she felt she had never grasped any lesson so thoroughly before: every little detail seemed impressed upon her memory, and she was quite sorry when the class came to an end, and Mademoiselle arrived to take French translation. Eleven o'clock was the signal for ten minutes' interval for lunch, and most of the girls began at once to leave the room. Patty was on the point of following, when a hand was laid on her arm, and turning round she saw Enid, the pretty dark-eyed girl who had eaten so many sweets in the train.

"I've been looking out for you ever since we got to school," said the latter. "What became of you yesterday? I didn't see even the end of your hair ribbon."

"I was having exams. nearly all day," answered Patty, "but I was in the recreation room in the evening. Didn't you see me?"

"No, of course I didn't, or I'd have come and spoken to you."

"I wish you had, then, for nobody spoke to me at all, and no one's said a word to me at meals, or in my bedroom either."

In spite of herself, Patty could not help her voice sounding rather aggrieved.

"What a shame! Then you don't know anybody at The Priory yet?"

"Only my cousin Muriel."

"Muriel Pearson? Is she your cousin?"

"Yes."

"Well!" exclaimed Enid, throwing such a depth of expression into the brief monosyllable, that it seemed to convey a whole volume of indignant comment.

"Do you actually mean to say," put in Avis, who had joined them, "that Muriel Pearson's your cousin, and yet she's never taken any notice of you, nor introduced you to anybody?"

Patty nodded. She did not want to accuse Muriel, but she certainly could not deny the fact.

"Then she's the meanest, nastiest girl in the whole school, and I shall just tell her so," said Enid, flushing quite scarlet with righteous wrath. "I never thought much of her, but I didn't believe she'd have done such a horrid thing as this. She deserves to be sent to Coventry for it."

"Didn't Miss Lincoln ask anybody to be friends with you?" enquired Avis.

"No; I only saw Miss Lincoln for a few minutes in the library when I came."

"That's queer, because she always sees that new girls are made to feel at home. But I expect she'd think your cousin would be sure to look after you. Oh, it's too bad! I can't forgive Muriel."

"Come with us to lunch, and we'll try and make up for it, at any rate," said Enid, seizing Patty by the arm, and dragging her down the passage to the pantry. "My name's Enid Walker, and this is Avis Wentworth. That's Winnie Robinson over there. Come here, Winnie, I want to tell you something. Do you know, this new girl is Muriel Pearson's cousin, and Muriel never introduced her to anybody, and she's not had a soul to talk to since she came. Isn't Muriel mean?"

"Disgusting!" cried Winnie; "but it's just like her. She and Maud Greening and Vera Clifford and Kitty Harrison have made a little set all to themselves, and they won't let anyone else come into it. Not that one wants to, I'm sure. I don't care to be friends with them in the least. You'd better drink your milk, Avis, if you want it. Be quick! The bell will ring in a moment. The bread and butter's all gone, I'm afraid."

"Never mind, I don't care for any. Why, talk of people and they're sure to turn up! Here she is!" replied Avis, as Muriel entered the pantry to replace her empty glass on the table.

"Muriel Pearson, there's something we want to say," began Enid. "The way you've treated your cousin is simply horrid. You ought to be thoroughly ashamed of yourself, and I hope you are."

Muriel raised her eyebrows and looked at Enid with an expression of supercilious surprise.

"Really, Enid Walker," she replied, "who asked you to interfere in my affairs?"

"Nobody, but I mean to, all the same. You deserve to be cut by the whole class, and I shan't be friends with you again."

"That's no great loss," said Muriel; "I wasn't aware that we ever were friends."

Her tone was disdainful, and the coolness of her manner contrasted strongly with Enid's excited indignation.

"But you were mean, Muriel," said Avis. "Why couldn't you introduce Patty to some of us?"

"It doesn't seem to have been necessary," replied Muriel; "you've evidently taken her up on your own account. I suppose Patty can make her friends, and I can have mine?"

"But you left her quite alone at first, with nobody to speak to," said Winnie; "it was most unkind. You weren't treated like that when you were a new girl. I remember taking you round the school myself."

"You've a better memory than I have, then," said Muriel. "I wish you'd all mind your own business. When I want to know your opinions, I'll ask for them." And she stalked out of the pantry with a very haughty look on her face, and without bestowing a glance on Patty.

"She needn't ask me to paint anything in her album, for I shan't do her even a pencil sketch!" declared Winnie.

"I wish I hadn't given her the rest of my chocolates! I wouldn't have done so if I'd known," said Avis.

"I'm glad she's not my cousin," said Enid; then, suddenly realizing that her remark was scarcely tactful, and that Patty was looking uncomfortable, she continued: "Never mind, Patty, we like you, you know. You shan't be able to say now that you haven't a friend in the school. I'm going to ask Miss Lincoln to let us each move up a little, so that you can sit next to me at dinner. I know Cissie Gardiner won't mind giving you her seat when I tell her the reason. There's the bell! I wish we could have our desks near each other, but Miss Harper won't let us change when once we've chosen places for the term. Be quick! We must fly, or we shall all lose order marks."

CHAPTER V

The Arithmetic Examination

PATTY's first letter home was, after all, a far more genuinely cheerful one than she had expected. She thought it better not to say anything about Muriel's behaviour, knowing it would greatly distress her father and mother, so only mentioned that she had made friends with her fellow-travellers in the train, and how much she liked them. To be included in such a pleasant set certainly made all the difference between happiness and unhappiness at The Priory. Enid seemed determined to make up to Patty for the neglect she had experienced at first, and took great pains not only to show her the ways of the school, but to see that she took her due part in the tennis sets and other games. Miss Lincoln had arranged the afternoon exercise as systematically as the morning lessons, with the object of obtaining as much variety as possible. Twice weekly the girls played hockey under the direction of Miss Latimer, the gymnastic mistress; twice also they were taken for walks in the neighbourhood; and on the remaining Wednesday and Saturday afternoons, which were regarded as half-holidays, they were allowed to amuse themselves as they liked, though they were required to be out-of-doors if the weather permitted. The judicious combination of work and play made the daily round both pleasant and healthy. The girls had enough lessons to keep them occupied, yet their brains were not over-taxed, and the hours spent in the open air ensured rosy cheeks and good appetites. When once she had settled down in her fresh surroundings, and the longing for home had become less keen, Patty found life at The Priory very congenial—whether in class, where Miss Harper made every subject so interesting; in the refectory, where she now sat in great content between Enid and Avis; or in the playing fields, where she was beginning to understand the mysteries of hockey, and to grow quite clever at putting, which was a favourite substitute for golf. She enjoyed the atmosphere of a large school, the little excitements, and the hundred-and-one topics of conversation which seemed continually to be discussed by those around her.

After having been the eldest at home, and the head pupil at Miss Dawson's, with so much to overlook and to arrange for others, it was quite a relief to find herself among the younger ones, and she would listen with enthusiasm to the speeches of the prefects in the debating society, and watch their prowess at hockey with never-failing admiration. She had not yet dared to speak to any of the big girls; but they seemed so clever and important in her eyes, that she felt pleased if she might only stand near while they were talking, and proud indeed if she happened to be included in the same team with some of them.

Naturally, her new life was not without its troubles. After Miss Dawson's easy methods, she found it needed all her energies to keep up to the high standard required by Miss Harper. She worked her hardest both in school hours and preparation, but even with her best efforts it was not always possible to win approbation from her teacher, and her most careful exercises were often returned with ruthlessly severe comments. Her companions in No. 7 were also uncongenial. They were themselves members of the Upper Fourth, and though they now spoke to her, and were to a certain degree more civil, they were not really nice and friendly, and often made her feel she was not wanted in the bedroom. They were willing enough to accept any of the kind little services which she was generally ready to perform, allowed her to tidy the room, to throw open the windows, to go to the bathroom to fetch the large can of hot water which was to be divided among the four basins; indeed, they began to depend so much upon her, that if a button needed stitching on hastily, a blouse fastening at the back, or a lost article must be searched for, they all said "Ask Patty", without the least hesitation, knowing that she would not refuse, and never seemed too busy to help other people. Of her cousin Patty saw little, and that little was unfortunately far from pleasant. Muriel seemed determined to show that although they might both be in the same school, and even in the same class, she did not intend to be compromised by their relationship. She was a very vain girl, who thought much of her parents' wealth and position. She considered Patty's advent would not bring her any great credit among the set of companions whom she had chosen, whose standard consisted mainly of pretty clothes and worldly possessions, and she was annoyed that her father should have wished to give her cousin the same advantages as herself. She lost no opportunity of slighting Patty, never by any chance sat next to her, always chose the opposite side in a game, and on many small occasions made herself actively disagreeable. Patty bore it as patiently as she could. She ventured once to remonstrate in private, but the result was so unfortunate, that she determined she would not try the experiment again. Evidently the only thing to be done was to acknowledge the estrangement, and to keep out of Muriel's way as much as possible. Her uncle's letter, however, weighed on her mind. How was she to prove her cousin's friend so entirely against her will? Poor Patty's conscience, always a tender one, even accused her of accepting Uncle Sidney's kindness without fulfilling his conditions, and she sometimes wondered whether she was justified in remaining at The Priory, when she was not able to play the part he had designed for her.

"And yet," she thought, "it's not my fault in the least. I'm ready any time to help her if she'll let me. Perhaps an opportunity may come some day, and in the meantime, however horrid she is to me, I won't say anything disagreeable back. That's one resolve I mean to stick to, at any rate, though it's hard sometimes, when she says such nasty things."

The Fourth Form seemed split up into a good many small sections. The lower division kept mostly to itself, and in the upper division there were several sets. Muriel and her three friends, for no good reason at all, considered themselves slightly superior to the rest of the class, and put on many airs in consequence, a state of affairs which was much resented by Enid Walker and Winnie Robinson, who, with Avis Wentworth, had a clique of their own, in which they now included Jean Bannerman and Patty. Doris Kennedy, May Firth, and Ella Johnson, the three girls who shared Patty's bedroom, made a separate little circle with Beatrice Wynne, while Cissie Gardiner and Maggie Woodhall were such bosom friends that they did not want anybody else's society. Patty found the liking she had taken to Jean Bannerman increased on further acquaintance. Jean was a most pleasant companion; she was interesting and sympathetic, and while ready enough for fun, was more staid and thoughtful than Enid, though the latter's amusing nonsense and bright, warm-hearted ways made her very attractive. Poor Enid was often in trouble; her lively tongue could not resist talking in class or whispering during preparation hours. She was ready enough to respect Miss Harper, but she was apt to defy Miss Rowe's authority, a form of insubordination which generally ended in disastrous consequences. Patty, in common with most of the class, found it rather difficult to get on with Miss Rowe. It felt hard to be corrected sharply for some slight slip, and to be expected to obey every trivial order as promptly as soldiers on parade duty. The girls resented the young teacher's imperious manner, and were sometimes on the verge of rebellion.

"She's only about five years older than we are," declared Enid, "if so much. I believe she's younger than my sister Adeline at home, so it's absurd to be expected to behave as if she were Miss Lincoln. She's really not much more than a monitress, although she's called a mistress."

"She makes so many tiresome, silly rules," said Winnie. "Miss Harper never thinks of telling us to sit with our arms folded, or all to open our books at exactly the same moment, and to place our pencils on the right-hand side of our desks. One feels like a kindergarten baby with Miss Rowe. She ought to teach children of six."

"I wish she didn't take arithmetic, at any rate," groaned Avis. "I never can get my sums right, especially those horrid problem ones she's so fond of. The more she explains, the more muddled I feel, and then she says I'm the stupidest girl in the class, and tells Miss Lincoln it's no use sending me in for the 'Cambridge', because she's sure I shouldn't pass."

"She's good at mathematics herself," said Winnie, "and she thinks that anyone who isn't hasn't got brains. All my problem sums were wrong yesterday, and I got a bad mark. I hope she won't put too many of them in the exam. to-day."

"If she does we'll go on strike, and say we can't do the paper. I can't possibly calculate where two people will meet each other on the road, if they start from different points at different times. I should think it depends how often they sit down to rest, or stop to talk to friends on the way, or how fast they want to get to the end of their journey," said Avis.

"There was that dreadful problem about dividing oranges among schoolboys," continued Winnie. "If I know anything of boys, they'd have thrown them down and scrambled for them; it would have been a far easier way of settling it. I always feel my head ache after trying to reckon those absurd things."

Every fortnight the class had a small examination in arithmetic, which was almost as solemn an affair as those held at the end of the term. Among other rules, Miss Rowe had decided that the girls, instead of remaining at their own desks, should all change places and sit according to her directions, her object being to separate those kindred spirits who, she considered, might be tempted to whisper or otherwise communicate with each other if left in too close proximity. By this new arrangement Patty found herself seated next to Muriel. Enid was at the desk behind, and it was therefore impossible to exchange even a smile with her without deliberately turning round. For some time the class worked away steadily and in silence. Occasionally a girl would so far forget herself as to count aloud, but a glare from Miss Rowe would instantly recall her to a sense of the enormity of such a misdeed. Naughty Enid managed to draw a cat on the margin of her blotting paper, and held it up for an admiring comrade to see; and Beatrice Wynne gave a terrific yawn, for which she was told to lose an order mark. Patty had been struggling for a long time with a difficult sum in compound proportion, and having just finished it, paused for a moment to take a rest. She presently became aware that Muriel, with lips pursed up as if forming the word "Hush!" was trying to attract her attention, and that Muriel's hand was secretly passing her a small note under cover of the desk. She opened it at once. It ran thus:

"How do you state Question 5? Ought the answer to be in bales of silk or days?"

Now Patty had only been a fortnight at The Priory; she knew little of the rules of a large school, and this was the first real class examination in which she had ever taken part. At Miss Dawson's school she was accustomed to help any girl who applied to her for aid, and indeed had often taught the younger ones how to work new rules, with the full sanction and approval of the mistress. She did not yet understand that an examination was a test of individual knowledge, and that no assistance must be either asked for or given. The only thing she realized was that Muriel wanted to know something which it was in her power to explain. She moved, therefore, as close to her cousin as she could, and, leaning over towards the latter's desk, took up her paper of questions.

"I've just finished it myself, and it comes out nicely in bales of silk," she whispered.

"Patty Hirst!" cried Miss Rowe, springing up in horrified indignation. "Do you know that any girl detected in the act of copying must instantly leave the examination?"

"Please, Miss Rowe, I wasn't copying," returned Patty, with some surprise.

"But I saw you deliberately look at your neighbour's paper."

"I wanted to show her something," explained Patty.

"Indeed!" said Miss Rowe incredulously. "You know perfectly well that all communication is strictly forbidden. Muriel, did you ask Patty anything?"

"I didn't speak at all, Miss Rowe," replied Muriel hastily.

"I am glad to hear it. Patty, take your papers at once and come to this table by the window. One of our first principles at The Priory is the strictest honesty in our work."

"But indeed I never intended——" began Patty.

"Do as you are told, or leave the room!" commanded Miss Rowe in her most decisive tone. "I cannot have the examination interrupted."

Patty gathered up her papers and obeyed in silence. She saw that she had been suspected of trying to cheat, and the injustice of the accusation was hard to bear. It was impossible to clear herself without involving Muriel, and she hated to tell tales. She felt it was too bad of her cousin thus to let her bear all the blame, for Muriel, even if she had not spoken, had put the question in writing, so that she had practically told an untruth to Miss Rowe when she denied any knowledge of the affair. Would the other girls in the class, Patty asked herself, also think she was trying to copy her neighbour's sums and gain an unfair advantage? To such an honourable nature the idea was terrible, and she longed to protest her innocence. Perhaps nobody would be friends with her any more if they believed her capable of such conduct, and she would be lonely again, as she had been at first. The little occurrence, though it only occupied a few minutes, completely disturbed the examination as far as she was concerned. She found it no longer possible to concentrate her mind on her sums. In the midst of adding up a column her thoughts were busy trying to imagine some explanation which might perhaps be given without betraying Muriel, and as no solution of the difficulty occurred to her, she found herself going over the same figures again and again without in the least realizing what she was doing. Matters, however, were not quite so desperate as she supposed.

Enid's sharp eyes had taken in the whole situation. From her seat behind she had seen Muriel hand the note to Patty, and had also noticed that the little piece of paper had fallen on to the floor underneath the desk. Putting out her foot, she managed to draw it nearer to her, then, dropping her pocket handkerchief, she stooped and picked up the two together, without anybody noticing that she had done so. She put the crumpled note with her handkerchief into her pocket, and went on with her examination, determined to sift the affair afterwards, and to take up the cudgels boldly on Patty's account. At eleven o'clock all papers were tied and handed in to Miss Rowe, and the girls filed out of the room. Enid saw Muriel glance cautiously at the floor under Patty's desk, as if searching for her note, and laughed to herself to think that she had already secured it.

"Are you looking for anything?" she asked, meaningly.

"Oh, dear, no!" returned Muriel. "At least, I thought I'd dropped a piece of indiarubber; but it doesn't matter, I've two or three others."

Enid waited a moment to let her pass, then, following, found all the class collected in a group outside the pantry door, talking over the examination and comparing the answers to the sums.

"What have you got for No. 5, Vera?" said Kitty Harrison. "Wasn't it a most horribly difficult one?"

"Dreadful! I couldn't do it at all. I got my statements in such a muddle, I had to leave it."

"What's your answer, Muriel?" asked Cissie Gardiner.

"270 bales of silk, but I don't believe it's right."

"Most of the others have 340 bales."

"Which others?"

"Why, Patty Hirst, and Beatrice Wynne, and Ella Johnson. Patty has most of her sums right, I think."

"She may well have," sneered Maud Greening, "if she copies other people's," she added under her breath.

"I don't even look at anyone else when I'm working," observed Muriel, pointedly.

"We've never had cheating in the Upper Fourth before," put in Vera Clifford.

"It's only the kind of thing one might expect, though," said Kitty Harrison. "Some people aren't as particular as we are."

Poor Patty, who was standing near, flushed red with indignation at these imputations, but did not know how to defend herself. Enid, however, flew to the rescue.

"Look here!" she cried. "If you've anything you want to say, I wish you'd say it straight out, instead of these back shots. If you think Patty was trying to cheat this morning, I can tell you you're much mistaken."

"Oh! you've taken up Patty Hirst," said Maud, "and of course you say she's always in the right. I'm afraid it's no use your trying to make excuses for her."

"I don't want to," declared Enid. "I only want the truth, and Muriel knows perfectly well that it was mostly her fault."

"I don't know anything about it," said Muriel. "I can't help people looking over my shoulder."

"Not when you ask them to!"

"I don't know what you mean."

"Copying is called sneaking in boys' schools," said Kitty Harrison.

"And so are other things," said Enid. "Look, girls! what do you think of this? I saw Muriel pass it to Patty during the exam."

She drew the piece of paper out of her pocket and handed it round for everybody to see. It was written in Muriel's rather peculiar handwriting, so there was no possibility of a mistake. There it was in black and white: "How do you state Question 5? Ought the answer to be in bales of silk or days?"

It was Muriel's turn now to flush red; she really had not a word to say for herself, and turned hastily away. Her three friends looked extremely blank, and Maud Greening murmured something about a mistake.

"Well," exclaimed Cissie Gardiner, "who talked about cheating, I should like to know?"

"And said it was called sneaking?" said Maggie Woodhall.

"I think some people can be very deceitful," said Winnie Robinson.

"She oughtn't to have been going to show Muriel how to work sums in the middle of the exam., though," said May Firth.

"She doesn't understand exams.; she never had them at her other school," explained Enid, "so she didn't really know she oughtn't. Did you, Patty?"

"Indeed I didn't," declared Patty. "I won't do such a thing another time."

"Well, there's a vast difference, at any rate, between wanting to help people and trying to copy their sums," said Winnie.

"I hope you all thoroughly understand the matter now," said Enid.

"If I were Patty I should want that note to be shown to Miss Rowe," suggested Cissie Gardiner.

"It's exactly what I'm going to do with it. Give it me back at once!" cried Enid. "Muriel thoroughly deserves to get into trouble."

"No, Enid, please don't; I beg you won't!" pleaded Patty.

"Why not?"

"Because I don't want you to."

"But why? Miss Rowe ought to hear about it."

"Oh, it really doesn't matter! Now that all of you know I didn't mean to cheat, I don't care. I hate tell-tales."

"I should care," declared Winnie.

"It's no use getting Muriel into trouble," said Patty.

"It would serve Muriel right," said Enid, indignantly. "Patty, you're a great deal too good-natured."

"No, I'm not. Please let me have the note, Enid."

"I don't think I will."

"But it's mine. It was written to me, remember."

Enid relinquished the incriminating piece of paper very reluctantly, and looked on with disfavour while Patty tore it to shreds.

"I'm fond of justice," she said, "and Muriel Pearson has got off too easily. Patty, I'm not sure if you're not a little too good for this world! I couldn't have torn that note up myself, and yet on the whole I like you for it. You're one of the nicest girls I've ever known!" And throwing her arm affectionately round Patty's waist, she walked with her along the passage to the classroom.

During an interval in the hockey practice that afternoon, Muriel found an opportunity to speak to her cousin.

"How stupid you were this morning, Patty!" she said. "What possessed you to lean over my desk and whisper?"

"What else could I do, when you'd asked me how to work that sum?" replied Patty.

"Why, of course you should have written me a note back, and handed it to me underneath the desk."

"But I'm afraid that wouldn't have been fair," objected Patty.

"Quite as fair as whispering."

"I didn't know either was wrong. You shouldn't have asked me."

"Oh, don't begin preaching to me! You contrived to make it very unpleasant for me, at any rate, and I shan't soon forget."

"Muriel! You know I never meant——"

"I don't care what you meant. Enid Walker has been telling Phyllis Chambers, and Phyllis won't put my name down for the hockey final. It's too bad."

"I'm dreadfully sorry."

"What's the use of being sorry? You should have managed better. I'm out of the match on Friday, and it's entirely your fault. I wish you'd never come to The Priory at all!" And Muriel walked away with such a sulky expression on her face, that no one at that moment would have called her pretty.

Patty knew it was no use trying to justify herself further. Muriel was determined to be angry, and having secured what she considered a grievance against her, would make that an excuse for avoiding her altogether. She could only hope that her cousin would not give a distorted version of the story in any of her letters home, and allow Uncle Sidney to believe that she had been unkind. That would indeed be most unjust, especially as she would have no opportunity of ever explaining the true facts of the case.

"She surely couldn't!" thought Patty. "It would be too untruthful. I hope she never mentions me at all when she writes. Oh, dear! How hard it is when you know you ought to be friends with someone and you can't! If only Muriel were Enid or Jean, how different it would be! I shouldn't have a single trouble left in the world, and life at The Priory would be just delightful."

CHAPTER VI

Albums

"I WANT you to put something in my album, Patty," said Winnie Robinson one afternoon, producing a dainty little volume reserved for souvenirs of her friends. "You're clever at drawing, so please let it be a picture, and if you can colour it, so much the better."

"I hope I shan't spoil your book," replied Patty, turning over the leaves to look at the various artistic efforts and poetical quotations with which about half the pages were filled.

"Of course you won't! I expect yours will be one of the nicest. I want every girl in the class to either paint or write something, and then I shall have a keepsake of the Upper Fourth. Maggie Woodhall drew this pretty little dog, and Ella Johnson those roses, and Enid has promised to make up a piece of poetry on purpose."

"It was only half a promise," declared Enid.

"Then you must write half a poem."

"Suppose the Muse deserts me?"

"Oh, rubbish! You can always make up verses. They seem to flow just as if you turned on a tap."

"Have you an album, Patty?" enquired Avis.

"No," said Patty. "I never saw one like Winnie's before. It's something quite new to me."

"Oh! then you must get one. They're the fashion just at present, and every girl in the class has one."

"We're rather fond of fads at The Priory," explained Winnie. "We have a rage for some particular thing, and are quite silly over it for a while, until we grow tired of it, and take up something else. This is about the fifth craze since I've been at the school. They never last long."

"The first was foreign stamps," said Enid. "Don't you remember how keen we were about collecting them, and how we envied May Firth because she had an uncle in Persia?"

"Maggie Woodhall got several stamps from Mexico," said Avis. "I think her collection was one of the best."

"I was very enthusiastic about mine," said Enid. "I exchanged three new lead pencils once for a Japanese stamp, and I asked Mother for an album for my birthday present. It was a beauty, too. Then, in the holidays, I went to stay with my godmother, and she had a whole pillow-case full of old letters, mostly foreign ones. She let me tear the stamps off all the envelopes, and I got at least twenty new kinds. I was delighted with them; but when I came back to school the fashion had changed, everybody was tired of stamps, and nobody cared to look at mine, so I gave the book to my brother. The boys in his class were collecting, and he was only too pleased to have it."

"I believe crests came next," said Avis reflectively. "Vera Clifford introduced them, because she was so proud her family has one of its own. She put it on the front page, and showed it to everybody."

"Yes, and she never forgave Doris Kennedy for making fun of it."

"What did Doris say?"

"Well, you see, the Clifford crest is a lion holding a shell, and the motto is a Latin one which means, 'Do not touch!' Doris said the lion was holding a purse, and the motto meant, 'What I've got I'll keep'. It was a good hit at Vera, because she's very stingy, although she has plenty of pocket money. She only gave twopence to the Waifs and Strays Fund—it was less than anybody else in the class; and she'll hardly ever lend her things, either, though she often borrows from other girls."

"She used all my Indian ink last term, and never gave me any back when she bought a new bottle," said Winnie. "She's certainly rather mean."

"The crests looked beautiful when they were pasted into albums," said Avis. "Beatrice Wynne used to paint borders round hers in red, and blue, and gold. Her book was like an old illuminated manuscript."

"It was a difficult craze, though, to keep up," said Winnie, "because we couldn't most of us collect enough crests to fill a book. Post-marks were much easier. We used to arrange them according to the different counties they were in. Miss Harper encouraged that fad; she said it taught us geography."

"So it did; but we made the most absurd mistakes sometimes. I remember putting Abingdon down under Devonshire, and Ilkley under Lincolnshire. I used to have to look the places up in the atlas. It was rather too like lessons to be very popular, so we all took to drawing pigs instead."

"Drawing pigs!" exclaimed Patty.

"Yes, with your eyes shut. It's most amusing to have a pig book. You get each of your friends to close her eyes tightly, and then draw a pig, putting in its tail and its eye, and to sign her name to it afterwards. You can't think what funny pictures people make. The eye's generally in the middle of the pig's back, and the tail twirling away anywhere but in the right place."

"All except Miss Harper's pig," said Winnie, "and that was because she drew the eye first. It wasn't quite fair, because you're supposed to put it in last of all; but of course none of us dared to tell her so. I have it in my book still, signed E.J.H.; it's got the most impertinent snout, and large peaked ears. I'm sure she must have been practising drawing pigs before she did it."

"Ghost signatures were nearly as much fun," said Enid.

"What are those?" enquired Patty, to whom all these schoolgirl pastimes were unknown.

"You have a special autograph book for them," explained Enid. "You double a page in half, and write your name inside exactly on the crease of the paper; then you fold the two halves together again without blotting it and press hard. It smudges your signature into such a queer shape. Everybody's comes out differently. One looks like a caterpillar, and another like a butterfly, or perhaps a fish's backbone. Ella Johnson's was the exact image of an oak tree."

"And Maud Greening's was like a pressed fern," said Winnie. "Do you remember the fad we had for pressed flowers and skeleton leaves? We used to keep them inside all our books."

"Yes, we soaked the leaves in water till they turned into skeletons. We pressed the flowers in blotting paper, and they were often lovely."

"Some of the girls were quite sentimental over them. Cissie Gardiner had a pansy picked from Wordsworth's garden at Grasmere, and a sprig of rosemary that she said came from the grave of Keats. Her aunt brought it to her from Rome, where he's buried. She pasted it on to a piece of paper, and wrote underneath: 'Here's rosemary, that's for remembrance. I pray you, love, remember.' She said Keats was her favourite poet. She thought it was so romantic for him to die so young of a broken heart, and she admired his portrait at the beginning of his poems, and if only she could have lived a hundred years earlier, then perhaps she might have known him."

"It was all Cissie's fault that we lost our collections," said Avis.

"What happened?" asked Patty, who found the reminiscences interesting.

"Well, we used to keep the leaves and flowers inside our books, and look at them during class whenever we had an opportunity. One day, during grammar, Cissie was sitting gazing at her piece of rosemary, and, I suppose, thinking of Keats, for she didn't hear when she was asked a question. Miss Rowe repeated it, and Cissie gave such a start that all her treasures fell from her book on to the floor. Miss Rowe looked very grim, and told her to pick them up, and ordered each girl to take every single leaf and flower out of her book also. Then she made Cissie collect them all, and fling the whole pile into the grate. Poor Cissie was in tears. She tried hard to save her sprig of rosemary: she begged Miss Rowe to let her keep it, and said she'd put it away in her drawer, and never bring it to class again; but Miss Rowe said she wouldn't encourage such nonsense, and the best place for it was the fire."

"It was just like Miss Rowe," said Enid; "she always uses what my father calls 'drastic measures'. Cissie's tired of Keats now. She's made a hero of

General Gordon instead, and has his portrait hanging up in her bedroom, with a piece of palm over it. She says she should like to marry a soldier some day, only she'd be so afraid of his getting killed."

"Cissie's a goose," said Winnie; "she can think of nothing but soldiers since her brother went to Sandhurst. She even drew one in my album, and it's not particularly well done. Patty, are you going to paint anything for me, or are you not? I'll leave the book with you for a week, and at the end of that time I shall expect to see something nice."

Patty was rather clever at drawing. She could copy very exactly, and even make original sketches sometimes. Mr. Summers, the art master, thought well of her work, and had praised her study of a group of apples more highly than those of the other girls. It was quite a consolation to Patty to excel in something. She found the afternoon spent in the studio the pleasantest in the whole week, and wished the drawing lessons came oftener. She was not without a secret hope that some of her work might be considered good enough to secure a place in the small exhibition of Arts and Crafts which was held yearly at the school, and to which only very creditable efforts were admitted. The neat drawings with which she illustrated her botany schedules were the admiration of her classmates, though they did not always meet with the appreciation from Miss Harper which they deserved. On one occasion Patty had taken immense trouble to copy a harebell as an example of the order *Campanulaceæ*. She had shaded it carefully in Indian ink, with very fine cross hatchings, and hoped it might win an extra mark, or at any rate a word of approbation. Disappointment, however, was in store for her. Miss Harper handed back the book with the remark:

"If you would spend less time on drawings, and more on the subject-matter of your exercises, Patty Hirst, I should be better satisfied with your work."

"It's so difficult to remember all those long, hard botanical terms," Patty complained afterwards to Jean. "I love the flowers, and I like to paint them and learn their English names, but I don't care in the least if their stamens are hypogynous or their cotyledons induplicate! I think it spoils them to pull them to pieces. They look so much prettier just as they're growing!"

The painting of a spray of honeysuckle which Patty did for Winnie was so beautifully done, that it was greatly envied by the other girls, all of whom begged for contributions to their own albums, and kept the little artist quite busy on half-holidays, or in any other leisure moments which she could spare. It was such a pleasant occupation that Patty did not grudge the time spent over it, and she was magnanimous enough to forget old grievances and to allow even Vera Clifford, Maud Greening, and Kitty Harrison to have specimens of her work, though Enid said they did not deserve it.

"They wouldn't any of them sit next to you when we were playing games last night," she declared, "and they were quite rude, and left you out altogether in the proverb questions. I think it is very cool of them to ask you. As for Muriel, I wonder she can bear to look at the lovely poppies you painted in her book, when she treats you so horridly."

It was Patty's birthday on the 24th of October, and for fully a week before that event she could not help noticing an unusual amount of mystery in the conduct of her friends. Several of them would be talking together with the greatest animation, and would drop suddenly into silence on her arrival. Enid twice began a sentence and stopped in the middle at a warning glance from Jean; and once, when Patty came unexpectedly into the classroom, there was a scuffle, the lid of Winnie's desk was banged down violently, and Winnie herself, together with Avis Wentworth and Cissie Gardiner, looked extremely conscious, as though they had been almost caught in some act which they wished to keep a secret. Patty wondered mildly why Enid seemed so anxious to ascertain whether she preferred red or blue, and whether she did not think a bright colour was always nicer than black; and she could not understand why her friend should one day be poring over a catalogue from the Stores, nor why she shut it up in such a hurry, remarking rather pointedly that Miss Lincoln had lent it to her.

"It's a queer book to choose!" laughed Patty. "I thought you were halfway through 'A Chaplet of Pearls'? I shouldn't think it's very amusing to read lists of groceries and household linen."

"On the contrary, I find it most interesting," replied Enid. "I never knew before how much shopping one could do at the Stores. They seem to have a department for everything."

On the morning of the birthday most of the members of the Fourth Class hurried away after breakfast with conspicuous haste. Patty stayed for a few minutes in the refectory to talk to some of the fifth class girls, and was in the middle of a conversation with Olive Hardman and Bella Ashworth, when Jean entered in search of her.

"Come, Patty," she said, "you're wanted in the classroom."

"Why, it's too early. It's only twenty-five minutes to nine," said Patty.

"Never mind. The girls are all there waiting."

"Waiting for what?"

"Waiting for you."

"Why for me?" asked Patty, in much surprise.

"Come along and you'll find the reason," replied Jean, taking her arm and leading her down the passage without further delay.

Considerably mystified at Jean's impatient hurry, Patty was still more astonished to discover the whole of both the Upper Fourth and the lower division collected round the fire in the schoolroom, and evidently anticipating her arrival with much eagerness.

"Here she is!" cried Jean. "Now, Enid, you can begin."

"We want to wish you very many happy returns of the day, Patty," said Enid, who seemed to be acting as mouthpiece for the rest. "And we hope you'll accept this birthday present; it's from us all."

"Thank you so much," said Patty, taking the offered parcel and beginning to untie the string. "I never expected that any of you would remember my birthday. Why, how lovely! Oh, it is good of you! The very thing in all the world I'd rather have than anything else."

The object which lay under the many folds of tissue paper was an album. It was bound in bright-blue morocco with gilt edges, and had smooth pages inside for writing, interleaved with pages of drawing paper for water colours. At the beginning was neatly printed:

PATTY HIRST

With love from the Fourth Class.

It was certainly a very appropriate present for the girls to have made, and one which Patty appreciated immensely. She had greatly longed to possess an album of her own, but had not liked to ask her mother to buy her one, and the beauty of this handsome gift far surpassed all her dreams.

"You'd done such lovely paintings in our books, that we felt we wanted to put something in yours," said Avis, "though I'm afraid our productions won't be very nice. I can't draw a stroke, and my writing's not at all elegant. I think you'd better not ask me."

In spite of Avis's protestations, Patty naturally asked her and the rest of the class for contributions, and the twenty-one souvenirs which resulted went a long way towards filling her volume. They varied much, both in quality and quantity, from Maggie Woodhall's fine pen-and-ink drawing to May Firth's washy little attempt at a landscape, or the short poetical quotation signed "Beatrice Wynne". Cissie Gardiner, always of a romantic turn of mind, copied "Has sorrow thy young days shaded?" from Moore's *Irish Melodies*, in her neatest handwriting. Naughty Winnie, who liked to make fun of Cissie, added a version of her own on the opposite page, which greatly destroyed the sentiment of the first, and provoked much laughter in the class. It ran thus:—

"Has sorrow thy young days shaded?
        Are schoolbooks and inkpots thy fate?
Too soon is thy fair face faded
        By working at Euclid so late.
Doth French thy bright spirit wither,
        Or Grammar thy happiness sear?
Then, child of misfortune, come hither,
        I'll weep with thee tear for tear."

"It's too bad!" said Cissie. "It spoils my verses; and Moore's my favourite poet just now. I like him far better than Keats; I think his pieces about soldiers and glory are simply splendid."

All the girls exerted themselves so much on Patty's behalf, that her album seemed to bring out an amount of talent lying dormant in the class which nobody had suspected before. Inspired by Winnie's original lines, several of the others set to work to make up verses, and the results were so satisfactory, that the authors felt themselves quite budding poetesses. Ethel Maitland, a quiet girl in the lower division, astonished everybody by the following composition, which was the more unexpected as nobody had ever considered her in the least clever.

TO PATTY

I thank the chance that doth afford
        Th' occasion fair and happy,
Upon this page to thus record
        My gratitude to Patty.
Within my album she hath wrought
        A picture of red roses,
All painted with most cunning skill,
        The prettiest of posies.
Had I but talent, in return
        A masterpiece I'd draw her,
But failing that, I pen these lines
        Which now I place before her.

"It's not very good," declared Ethel. "It was so hard to make it scan properly. I know 'happy' and 'Patty' don't really rhyme, but what else could I put? The last line's rather tame, but then again I couldn't find a rhyme for 'draw her'. I thought at first of putting 'And hope they will not bore her', or 'To show how I adore her', but perhaps it's better as it is."

Patty, who had no talent for poetry, was immensely impressed by these lines. She showed them to everybody in the class, and Ethel's work was much admired until it was entirely eclipsed by a contribution from Jean Bannerman. Jean had drawn a funny picture of a kitten with a pile of books under its arm. She had copied it from a magazine, but the verse which she wrote under it was her own composition. She called it:

AN ENTHUSIAST

> Her head well stored with copious knowledge,
> Miss Fluffy Purrem goes to College,
> Secure that never yet she's failed.
> Her subjects will not be *cur*tailed:
> On *cat*acombs she'll wax ecstatic,
> Yet much objects to be *dog*matic.
> She's great on ornithology,
> And also on astrology;
> She lets the Dog Star go astray,
> But revels in the *Milky Way*.
> She claims the *Manx* to be a nation,
> And holds strong views about cre(a)mation;
> At *Mew*nham they declare she's sure
> A first-class try*puss* to secure.

This delighted the girls, because the kitten's face really looked a little like Patty's, which was round too, and what Jean described as "purry",—"that's to say, looking pleased at everything, as if she were purring," she explained.

Enid had reserved her efforts until the last, and her page in the album was considered the very best of all. It was headed by a picture which was a curious notion of her own. When glanced at casually it might be taken for a sketch of a crocodile, but when examined closely it showed that the body was made up of girls walking along two and two, the smaller ones tapering down in height, and vanishing in the distance to form the tail. Though the details were not particularly well drawn, the whole effect was wonderfully good, and as "crocodiling" was the popular term at The Priory for walking two and two, the idea was most appropriate. Enid described it in the accompanying verses:

THE BALLAD OF THE SWEET CROCODILE

Oh! haven't you heard of the sweet crocodile?
It lives in the mud on the banks of the Nile.
'Neath the tropical sunshine it sits with a smile,
And feeds on the niggers who live by the Nile.
Oh, the sweet crocodile! The sweet crocodile!
It lives in the mud on the banks of the Nile.

But if you must live in this cold British isle,
It's not often you'll meet with the sweet crocodile.
The specimens here are as far as they're few,
And we treasure them carefully up in the Zoo.
Oh, the sweet crocodile! The sweet crocodile!
It doesn't thrive well in this cold British isle.

Yet if about Morton you'll walk for a mile,
You may see an uncommonly sweet crocodile.
It looks very neat, with its trim little feet,
And the people all smile when the creature they meet.
Oh, the sweet crocodile! The sweet crocodile!
It walks about Morton for many a mile.

But if you'll examine this sweet crocodile,
You'll see it's composed all of girls in a file.
And there's one, who's called Patty, with such a sweet smile,
That the people all rave on this sweet crocodile.
Oh! this Patty of mine, with the extra sweet smile,
She's a gem in the tail of the sweet crocodile.

This proved by far the most popular of all the contributions to Patty's album, and as numerous girls from other classes asked to look at the crocodile picture, the book was in danger of too much wear and tear, and at Miss Harper's suggestion it was placed temporarily in the school museum, so that everybody might have a chance of seeing it, yet it should be safe from careless hands. Enid was, of course, asked after this to compose so many poems for so many various albums, that had she consented her collected effusions might have filled a volume; but she steadfastly declined.

"I made this up specially for Patty, and on purpose to try and make her album a little different from anybody else's," she declared. "If I wrote verses and drew pictures for you all, there'd be nothing particularly out of the common about this. I don't intend to do a single thing for one of you, so please don't ask me again, for I shall only go on saying 'No'."

CHAPTER VII

Patty's Pledge

November days found Patty thoroughly settled down at The Priory, and quite accustomed to all the rules and regulations which obtained there. On the whole she was happy, but there were still a few difficulties with which she had to contend. Life in a large school, among so many companions of various dispositions, was a totally different affair from what it had been in her quiet home at Kirkstone. Though Miss Lincoln did her uttermost to uphold an extremely high standard of conduct among the girls, Patty found there were many who were capable of little meannesses, slight lapses from the strictly straight path, and acts which were not at all in accordance with her ideals of honour. It sometimes needed a good deal of moral courage to keep to what she knew was right. It was not pleasant to be laughed at and called "straitlaced", because she would not evade rules or join in certain doubtful undertakings. No one liked fun more than Patty, when it was open and above-board, but she could not bear to be mixed up in anything which seemed sly or underhand. In her bedroom particularly she found cause of trouble. Her three companions, Ella Johnson, May Firth, and Doris Kennedy would get up after Miss Rowe had made her evening rounds, relight the gas, and read storybooks in bed, a proceeding which was, of course, absolutely forbidden. They were quite angry with Patty when she ventured to remonstrate.

"We're not going to have you interfering with us, Patty Hirst. If we like to light the gas again we shall do so," said May.

"But if Miss Rowe catches you, you'll get into the most terrible scrape," said Patty.

"She won't catch us; we're too careful. I can put the gas out in a second if anyone's coming."

"You might find you had put it out a second too late, and what would you do then?"

"It will be quite time enough to decide when it happens," said Doris. "Don't bother! You can go to sleep yourself, if you want to, but we three mean to enjoy ourselves."

Patty, however, found it impossible to go to sleep. She lay awake, listening anxiously, afraid of hearing Miss Rowe's step in the passage, and wondering what the consequences would be if it were discovered that the occupants of No. 7 were astir after 9.30 p.m.

"Somebody might be walking through the garden and see a light in the window," she suggested to the others. "Suppose it were Miss Lincoln herself! How dreadfully angry she'd be!"

"Miss Lincoln's always safely in her study at this time," said May. "No one's in the least likely to interrupt us, or to know anything about it, unless you're mean enough to tell."

"You know quite well I'm no tell-tale," said Patty, indignantly. "You've nothing to fear from me. I only wish you wouldn't do it. Why can't you read the books downstairs? You've plenty of time after prep."

"Because Miss Rowe'd take them away. We're only allowed to have books from the school library, and these are some that Doris brought with her from home. They're most exciting. I simply must finish mine."

"Oh, May, that's worse than ever!" exclaimed Patty, "if they're books you know you oughtn't to read."

"Please be quiet, and mind your own business, Patty Hirst!" cried May, angrily. "We're not going to ask your leave for everything we do."

May, Ella, and Doris knew perfectly well that they were in the wrong, but they tried to justify their conduct to each other by calling Patty "priggish". They treated her in as cool a manner as possible, and generally had some secrets to whisper about in a corner of the room, making her feel how little they cared for her company, and how much they would have preferred Beatrice Wynne in her place. Patty, who hated quarrels, and would rather have been on friendly terms with everybody, disliked these unpleasant bickerings with her room mates; but as she would not yield her point, and they would not relinquish their practice, she had perforce to remain on rather distant terms with them. In school, too, she found that everything was not quite what might have been desired. Several of the girls helped each other openly with their French composition. They would meet together before class and compare sentences, hastily correcting errors, and copying each other's work to such an extent that one essay was simply a duplicate of the other, faults and all. Mademoiselle was not a very observant person, and in consequence never discovered what was taking place, though the similarity in the mistakes might easily have aroused her suspicions. The history exercises also gave wide scope to those who were not absolutely scrupulous. Miss Harper left much to the girls' sense of honour, trusting them completely, and never subjecting them to the strict surveillance which was practised by Miss Rowe. As a rule her plan met with excellent results, though unfortunately her confidence was sometimes abused. At the end of each chapter in the history book were a number of questions, which were given as a weekly exercise. The class was supposed to prepare the chapter first, then, opening the book at the page of questions, to write the answers entirely from memory.

A few did so, but I fear a large proportion of the girls yielded to the temptation thus placed in their way, and would take surreptitious peeps to supply missing dates or names. It seemed hard that the conscientious ones should often be obliged to lose marks, while those whose standard of right was lower won words of approval from Miss Harper for their correct exercises. Patty's particular friends—Enid, Winnie, and Jean—were among those to whom honour meant more than marks; but Avis, who was a much weaker character, sometimes allowed herself to slip, condoning her conduct by telling herself that everybody else did the same. Avis was seated close to Patty one morning during the half-hour allowed for the writing of the history exercise. She was not well prepared, and she was just refreshing her memory from the forbidden chapter, when suddenly she caught Patty's frank blue eyes fixed upon her with such a surprised and reproachful gaze, that she flushed scarlet with shame, and turned the pages of her book hastily back to the questions.

"I really never thought about it," she explained to Patty afterwards; "at least I suppose I did think, but I knew all the others were looking up what they had forgotten, so I supposed it didn't matter."

"Enid never looks," said Patty, gravely.

"Well, I won't do it again; I won't indeed."

"I was wondering," said Patty, "if we couldn't get up a little society, and ask the members to take a pledge to be absolutely honest about our lessons. Would you join?"

"Of course I would," said Avis, heartily. "I'd be very glad to. So would many of the girls, I'm sure. We all hate being unfair, only it seems too bad when two or three take an advantage and get the best marks."

Patty set to work without further delay, and managed to enrol thirteen names on her list of honour. Enid, Winnie, and Jean were naturally willing recruits, as were also Cissie Gardiner, Maggie Woodhall, and five of the lower division, including Ethel Maitland. Beatrice Wynne, after a little hesitation, added her signature, but May Firth, Doris Kennedy, and Ella Johnson refused point-blank.

"It's just another of your absurd fads, Patty Hirst," said Ella. "You're quite a new girl, it's only your first term here, and I think it's very conceited of you to be always trying to make out you're so much better than anyone else."

"Oh, Ella, you know I don't!" said poor Patty.

"Yes, you do," snapped Ella.

"You're not a monitress, Patty Hirst," said May Firth, "so I can't see why you should concern yourself with our affairs."

"Do your own exercises, and leave us to do ours," said Doris Kennedy. "We don't want to belong to your silly society."

After meeting with such a rebuff, Patty felt very diffident about mentioning the matter to the remaining members of the class. She had no wish to be considered self-righteous and interfering, but, all the same, she thought she was bound to try and use her influence to set straight what was certainly a doubtful practice, and she meant to persist even at the risk of being called hard names. She found Muriel and her three friends alone in the recreation room one afternoon, and screwed up her courage sufficiently to broach the subject to them.

"I wasn't aware that anybody cheated," said Muriel coldly, pausing for a moment in the letter she was writing. "If they do, by all means get them to take your pledge. It doesn't concern me."

"Nor me either," said Vera. "I go my own way, and don't trouble about other people."

"We thought perhaps you'd join, as so many of the girls have done so," said Patty, timidly.

"It's quite unnecessary," said Vera, "and for Maud and Kitty too. You'd better take it to the Fifth Class."

Kitty Harrison said nothing, but she came to Patty afterwards and asked that her name might be placed on the list.

"I think I can persuade Maud too," she said; "only you must promise faithfully not to let Vera or Muriel know anything about it. I'm glad you've got it up, Patty, because we all did really look back at the chapter in the history exercises, even Vera, though she won't confess it. Nobody will dare to cheat now that so much notice has been taken of it, and we'd all rather not, if everyone else will keep square. I always felt dreadfully mean, only I didn't like losing marks."

It was a great triumph for Patty to have won both Kitty and Maud to her side, and she had the added satisfaction of afterwards securing the two members of the lower division who had at first refused. Thanks to her exertions, the standard of the class seemed undoubtedly raised, and the Fifth Form girls, who shared the recreation room, and heard most of what was going on, took up the idea, and formed a society of their own. It was as if Patty had cast a stone into a smooth pond, and the ripples were spreading in an ever-widening circle. Without in the least realizing it, her school-fellows were influenced by her pleasant, sunny, unselfish ways. She had set a fashion of doing little kind, considerate, helpful things, which many of the rest began unconsciously to follow. There are always a large number of girls in a school who drift along without any special aim, yet are ready enough to respond to anyone who draws out the best that is in them. If one companion succeeds in avoiding little evils and inconsistencies, keeping her temper, and showing forbearance and self-restraint in all the small daily acts, her character will begin to invade other lives, and uplift them in spite of themselves. Patty was not aware that she had made any difference at The Priory, and certainly never for a moment intended to set herself up as an example; but without knowing it she had given a helping hand to several who, but for her, might never have made any endeavour to mount to a higher level. Avis in particular was far more conscientious than before, and Enid, who had hitherto been content if her half-learnt lessons did not win a scolding from Miss Harper, began to put more zeal into her work. She was a bright girl, and could easily win class laurels if she wished, though she disliked any continuous efforts. Her essays were full of originality, and she was quick at understanding anything which required reasoning, but she had little patience for remembering dates and facts, and was not capable of Patty's steady plodding. Though both Maud Greening and Kitty Harrison had become more friendly, Vera Clifford and Muriel still held aloof from Patty, and it was owing to them that an unpleasant incident occurred one day which caused the latter much distress. Patty's talent for drawing was well known in the school; she was clever at portraits, and with a few rapid lines could make excellent likenesses. The girls were fond of asking her to do sketches for them on scraps of paper, which they would afterwards keep inside their lesson books as great treasures. Among others, Patty had drawn a capital picture of Miss Rowe, showing her classical features and her coils of smooth, fair hair. It was regarded as her masterpiece, and Cissie Gardiner, its lucky owner, was quite envied by the rest of the class. Cissie placed it inside her *Merchant of Venice*, and for several days rejoiced in its possession. One morning, however, the Upper Fourth was reading Shakespeare with Miss Rowe. This lesson was always held in the lecture-room instead of in the classroom, where Miss Harper was teaching the lower division, and the girls sat on chairs arranged in a semicircle round their mistress. Cissie could not resist taking a peep at her portrait, and handed it to her neighbour to admire, who passed it on to the next girl, so that in course of time it found its way down the class to Vera Clifford. Now Miss Rowe was rather handsome, but she happened to have a scar down the side of her forehead, which slightly spoilt her good looks. Patty had naturally left this out in her sketch, but Vera, who had not the same nice feeling, took a pencil and, nudging Muriel, who sat next to her, put in the mark, which showed only too plainly across the brow.

"What are you doing? Pass it back at once!" whispered Cissie anxiously.

Her ill-judged concern, however, had the unfortunate effect of calling Miss Rowe's attention to the piece of paper.

"What have you there, Vera?" she asked.

Vera tried to hand the sketch back quickly to Maud Greening, and Maud made a valiant effort to slip it inside her Shakespeare; but as Maggie Woodhall happened at that instant to jog her elbow, she dropped the book, and the paper fluttered on to the floor, almost at the teacher's feet. Miss Rowe picked it up and looked at it critically.

"To whom does this belong?" she enquired sharply.

"It's mine, Miss Rowe, please," said Cissie.

"Did you draw it?"

"No, Miss Rowe."

"Then who did?"

"Patty Hirst," said Cissie, who had not seen Vera's alteration, and thought the portrait so flattering and talented that she saw no reason for withholding the artist's name, and, indeed, considered Patty might well be proud of such an achievement.

"Then I think Patty Hirst might employ her time more profitably," said Miss Rowe, and, turning very pink, she tore the picture across, and threw it into the waste-paper basket.

Cissie rescued the fragments afterwards, and pieced them together, and when she discovered the addition which had been made, her wrath and indignation knew no bounds. As for Patty, she was nearly heart-broken at the affair. She genuinely liked Miss Rowe, and could not bear her to think that she would have been so cruel and indelicate as to call attention to her one blemish. Even Vera was penitent, for though she had had the bad taste to alter the drawing, she certainly had not intended it to fall into the hands of the mistress herself. The hard part of it was that no one liked to explain, because to refer to it at all would only have seemed to make matters worse; so the girls consoled Patty as best they could, but it was a long time before she could get over it. Perhaps on the whole the occurrence made Vera a little less nasty to Patty. She was a proud, but not altogether an ungenerous girl, and she was genuinely sorry to have thus thrown blame on undeserving shoulders. But for Muriel's influence she would have been almost ready to follow the example of Kitty and Maud, and if not to make friends, at least to treat with tolerance a companion who was so particularly inoffensive, and so willing to meet an apology halfway.

The war which Patty waged in her bedroom still went on as before. Every night one of her companions would relight the gas, in spite of all entreaties. Sometimes Patty would get up and turn it out, greatly to the wrath of the others, who would retaliate next day by hiding her brush and comb, or dropping her cake of soap into her water jug. It was a most unpleasant state of affairs, and seemed likely to continue indefinitely, when an incident fortunately happened which led to a truce.

One November afternoon, when the girls were returning from hockey, Patty, in strolling through the shrubbery, noticed that the gardener, who had probably been unstopping one of the gutters, had left his ladder leaning against a wall, thus giving access to the flat roof of the lecture hall. Patty at home had sometimes been called a tomboy, and she could not resist climbing up to see what the world looked like from the top. She had reached the leads, and was on the point of stepping over a large spout, when she heard the sound of laughter on the roof, and stopped to listen. Someone was evidently already there, and, recognizing the voices of Doris, May, and Ella, she decided not to follow them. An idea had suddenly occurred to her, and acting upon it at once she descended to the ground, then, very gently removing the ladder, she laid it at the foot of the wall. The gardener's wheelbarrow, full of dead leaves, stood conveniently near, under the shelter of a large rhododendron, so she sat down on it, and waited for what she knew was bound to happen. I believe there was a little mischief in her eyes, for Patty liked a joke as well as anybody, and she thought the occasion offered considerable opportunities for fun. She had not to wait long. In a few minutes her three room mates, who had explored the roof as far as they dared to venture, returned to the spot where they had left the ladder, and were much astonished to find it gone.

"What a nuisance!" said May. "Ward must have taken it without our hearing him. I wonder where he is?"

"We shall have to call," said Ella; "perhaps he hasn't gone very far."

None of the three noticed Patty, who was hidden by the rhododendron, though by peeping through the leaves she was able to see them perfectly well.

"Coo—e—e!" cried Doris, as loudly as she could.

"Cuckoo!" shouted May, hoping some passing companion might be within earshot.

"What are we to do?" said Ella, when their calls had been repeated several times without rousing the faintest reply.

It was rather a lonely part of the garden; most of the girls had run from the hockey field straight into the house, and the gardener was at that moment partaking of tea in the kitchen. Patty, who had counted on all these points, remained quietly under cover, and suppressed her laughter as best she could.

"I don't know; we can't possibly jump it," said May, peeping over the edge to judge the distance between herself and the ground, and drawing back with a shudder.

"We shall have to wait till Ward comes back," said Doris.

"Suppose he's put the ladder away, and doesn't intend to come back?" suggested Ella.

"Then we'll have to stay here all night," said May.

"Oh, rubbish!" cried Doris. "Let us give one more good call; somebody's sure to come."

The combined efforts of three pairs of lungs raised a lusty shout, but beyond a slight echo there was no response.

"It's getting so dark. It must be almost tea-time, I'm sure," groaned Ella.

"They'll miss us at tea, I expect," said Doris.

"Yes, but they won't know where to look for us. They'll hunt in every place except the right one. No one would ever dream we were on the roof," said May dismally.

"Call again," said Ella, who was waxing tearful.

"Cuckoo!" tried May once more, with a tinge of despair in her voice.

This time Patty judged it discreet to come to the rescue, and emerging quietly from the shade of the rhododendron on the far side, she strolled up in a casual manner.

"Why, what are you three doing there?" she exclaimed, with well-feigned surprise.

"Oh, Patty! is that you?" cried Doris, with great relief. "Ward has taken away the ladder and we can't come down. I wish you'd go and fetch him."

"He hasn't taken the ladder away; it's lying on the ground under the wall," replied Patty.

"Then put it up for us, that's a sweet girl," said Ella, in a far more civil tone than she generally used.

"I don't know, on the whole, that I will," answered Patty.

Her three companions gasped.

"Why not?" asked Doris.

"Don't tease, Patty! It's getting dark and cold," said May.

"Do be quick, Patty!" said Ella.

"It would be colder still if you spent the night there," said Patty. "Think how nice it would be for me, though, to have the bedroom all to myself!"

"Patty, you can't really mean to leave us here!"

"If I put the ladder up, I shall expect something in return," declared Patty.

"All right. Go on. What do you want?"

"You'll all three have to promise never to light the gas again after Miss Rowe's turned it out, and not to read books that aren't allowed."

"Don't be stupid, Patty; we've argued that point so often."

"YOU'LL ALL THREE HAVE TO PROMISE NEVER TO LIGHT THE GAS AGAIN AFTER MISS ROWE'S TURNED IT OUT"

"Very well," said Patty, briefly, pretending to walk away.

A despairing wail from the girls, however, brought her back.

"Don't go! Won't you take anything else?" entreated Doris.

"Not a single thing," said Patty, firmly.

"How mean you are!"

"There's the tea bell," said Patty. "You'd better decide quickly, because I can't wait."

"Suppose we promise only to read books out of the library," began Ella, "and light the gas sometimes?"

"Good-night!" replied Patty, turning this time as if she really meant to go.

"We'll promise! We'll promise!" cried the three shivering figures on the roof.

"Everything?"

"Yes, if you like."

"On your honour?"

"On our honour."

"Never again?"

"Never."

"It's a bargain, then. Now you may all come down."

Patty reared the ladder against the wall, and held it steady while her companions descended. She felt in good spirits, for she had enjoyed the fun of keeping them imprisoned, and had been able by guile to extort a promise which her strongest protests had hitherto failed to gain from them.

"They don't know I hid the ladder," she said to herself as they all hurried in to tea, "and I don't mean to tell them. It's a grand victory for me. I shall hold them strictly to their word, and now at last we shall have a little peace in No. 7, and I shan't have to lie awake every night listening in fear and trembling for Miss Rowe."

CHAPTER VIII

A Great Disappointment

As December passed by, and the term drew to a close, Patty's impatience began almost to get the better of her. No thirteen weeks had ever appeared so long. She felt as if she had been away from home for years, and she yearned for a sight of all the loved faces. Letters, though very well in their way, were unsatisfactory things, especially the children's, which contained little news for the amount of paper covered, and consisted mostly of wishes for her return, with a whole page of crosses meant to represent kisses at the end. Now at last, however, she could count the remainder of the term by days instead of weeks, and her fancy was busy painting in rainbow colours a picture of her arrival, first at the station, where perhaps her father would meet her, and then at the dear, well-known door, where her mother would be waiting to clasp her in the warmest hug, and all the younger ones would be watching eagerly to welcome her back again. It was such an enthralling prospect that Patty's eyes shone whenever she thought about it, and she sometimes executed a little dance of delight in the privacy of her cubicle, to let off some of the effervescence of her spirits.

"Only four days more!" she said to herself one night. "I suppose I shall manage to get through them somehow! I wonder if it seems as long to Mother and the others! I've never looked forward to anything so much in my life. It makes me wild with joy to think it's so near."

Poor Patty! In the midst of her pleasant anticipations a bitter disappointment was in store for her. It seemed hard indeed that all her cherished plans must suddenly and ruthlessly be destroyed; but it takes a mingled warp and woof of joy and sorrow to weave the patterns of our lives, and a piece of dark background is sometimes needed to bring the brighter parts into full relief. The very next morning a letter arrived from Mrs. Hirst, containing such bad news that Patty had to read it twice over before she entirely grasped the full meaning of its tidings. Three of the younger children were ill with scarlet fever, Rowley seriously so, and Robin and Kitty quite poorly enough to cause a certain amount of anxiety. The small patients had been carefully isolated, and so far the other children were well; but they were of course liable to develop the complaint, and needed careful watching. In the circumstances it was quite impossible for Patty to come home. She must not venture within danger of infection, for even if she did not take scarlet fever herself, it would not be right to allow her to go back to school after the holidays from a house where there had been sickness.

"Uncle Sidney and Aunt Lucy have very kindly invited you to Thorncroft," wrote Mrs. Hirst, "so you will return with Muriel, and will, I hope, have a pleasant holiday there. It is hard for us all to miss our Christmas together, but you must be a brave girl, darling, and look forward to seeing us at Easter instead. I cannot even write to you often, because I am nursing our invalids, and Father has to disinfect my letters carefully in the surgery before he considers it safe to forward them. Milly, however, shall write you a postcard every day, to say how we are, and you will be constantly in my thoughts, though I may not be able to do more than send you a brief message."

To Patty it seemed as if the sun had suddenly gone out. That she must forego all her home joys and spend the holidays with Muriel was indeed a great hardship.

"Muriel won't want me, I know," she sobbed, "and it won't seem like Christmas at all to have to spend it at Thorncroft. Oh, how I wish I could have gone home first, before the children were taken ill, and then I could have helped to nurse them! Easter is months and months off. I don't know how I'm going to live till I see them all again."

After one storm of grief, however, Patty, like a sensible girl, dried her eyes, and tried to put on a bright face and make the best of things as they were. It seemed no use bemoaning her misery, and spoiling all her friends' happiness by dwelling on her troubles, so she managed to interest herself in Enid's packing, and to sympathize with Jean's choice of Christmas presents, though it was hard to listen to the others' glad plans when her own had suffered such shipwreck. It is a great accomplishment to be able to smile outside when we are crying inside, and I don't believe Patty could have done it if she had not been so accustomed to forget her own side of a question, and engross herself in other people's affairs. As it was, her power of self-mastery helped her to be brave and cheery in spite of her disappointment; but it was not an easy task, and it cost her best efforts to smother her grief, and keep up to anything like her usual level of good spirits. It is sometimes more difficult to practise the little self-denials and do the unlauded acts of courage than to make one supreme sacrifice while the world applauds; so I think Patty deserved to be called a heroine for her small victory, which nobody noticed, just as much as if it had been a great one. She had, at any rate, one compensation to console her. Jean Bannerman also lived at Waverton, and would travel home with Muriel and herself, and she hoped it might be possible to see something of Jean during the holidays. The breaking-up day arrived at last, and Patty, after a warm good-bye to Enid, Winnie, and Avis, was put with her two companions under the guardianship of Miss Rowe, who escorted them to the junction, and saw them safely into the northern express. Even though she was not going to her own home, Patty felt rather cheered at leaving The Priory and starting upon a journey; and the prospect of Christmas and its attendant festivities was an enlivening one.

She had a kind welcome from her uncle and aunt, and her cousin Horace, who had returned from school the day before, also seemed pleased to see her. Patty always liked Horace much better than Muriel. He was far kinder to her, and would often ask her to help him with his photography, or to arrange his cases of beetles, butterflies, and moths, entertaining her the while with accounts of his adventures at school, some of which were of such a thrilling description that she suspected they were made up for her benefit. Muriel, who preferred to keep her brother to herself, was jealous of this intimacy; she did not want to include Patty in their family life, and though she did not dare to say so to her parents, she secretly resented her cousin's presence. The two girls were necessarily thrown much in each other's company, and so overbearing did Muriel prove sometimes, that it needed all Patty's self-restraint to prevent a quarrel. It was not pleasant to be ordered about, told to fetch and carry, and receive no thanks for her pains; and particularly disagreeable to be given to understand that she was an unwelcome visitor, who ought to consider herself very fortunate to have been asked at all. Neither Mr. nor Mrs. Pearson had any idea how unkind Muriel was to Patty in private; they were proud of their pretty little daughter, and fondly liked to think she was everything they could desire: their love made them blind to small indications of character, and so long as they saw no glaring fault they thought all was well. Muriel from her babyhood had been accustomed to expect her own way in everything. Her father, mother, and brother had made a pet of her, and spoilt her so entirely that she had grown up a very selfish girl, and even the influence of school life, wholesome though it was, had not been able so far to undo the ill effects of her home training. The first few days at Thorncroft were naturally occupied with preparations for Christmas. Patty was very anxious to send some little gifts home to the children, and spent much time and thought planning how she could most advantageously lay out the few shillings of pocket money which she possessed. It was a difficult matter when there were so many presents required, and one which demanded serious consideration. In lack of any other confidant, she talked it over with Muriel.

"There's the tray-cloth for Mother, which I worked at school," she said. "That's quite finished, and it looks very nice, only a little crushed. Aunt Lucy says Emma shall iron it out for me. I wish I could think of something for Father. Can you suggest anything?"

Muriel shook her head.

"I can't," she replied. "I'm in the same difficulty nearly every year. There seems nothing you can give to a gentleman that he really cares for. I've made shaving cloths, and cigarette cases, and match-box holders, and heaps of other things for Father, and he always says 'Thank you!' and puts them away in his drawer, and never uses them. He must have a whole pile of my presents somewhere."

"I thought of a blotter," said Patty, "but I know it would only be left lying about in the surgery. Father has a stylo. pen, and hardly ever needs blotting-paper. The little ones give him useful things—boxes of matches, and railway guides, and cakes of soap."

"Cakes of soap!" laughed Muriel.

"Yes, why not? They can't think of anything else to buy. But I wanted something nicer. I wish someone would publish a book on how to make Christmas presents for one's father."

"They might suggest things, but they couldn't guarantee his using them when they were made."

"It's much easier for the children," said Patty, "because I know exactly what they'd like."

"That's no trouble, then," yawned Muriel. "We shall be going into town to-morrow. You'll have plenty of choice at Archer's."

"Too much, I'm afraid," said Patty. "I shall want to buy all I see."

"Well, if I were you, I should get them each a shilling toy, and then one wouldn't be better than another," said Muriel carelessly, rising and putting an end to a conversation of which she was growing tired. "I'm thankful to say my presents are all arranged."

It was easy enough, Patty thought, for Muriel to suggest shilling toys in such an airy manner, but quite an impossibility to provide them for seven brothers and sisters when her small green purse only contained a half-crown and a new sixpence. Her gifts would have to be very modest ones, and it would take much ingenuity to make her money last out. Emma, her aunt's maid, came to the rescue by hunting out a large bag of coloured wools and helping her to make a ball for the baby. This Patty knew would delight him, and would leave her a little extra to spend upon the others. On the day before Christmas Eve, Mrs. Pearson took Muriel and Patty to town with her, and after visiting several places, the carriage finally drew up at Archer's, a large general store where toys and all kinds of fancy articles were sold. The shop was so crowded that it was quite difficult to obtain attention from the overworked assistants, and Mrs. Pearson was obliged to wait some time before making her purchases. It had been a busy morning for her; she was not strong, and by the time she had bought what she needed, she was thoroughly tired.

"You children must be quick, if there is anything you want," she said, consulting her watch. "I particularly wish to be home by half-past twelve, so I can only allow you ten minutes for your shopping. Where shall we go first?"

"To the book department," said Muriel promptly. "You know I haven't spent the present Aunt Ida sent me yet, and I want to choose something nice."

"Wouldn't it do another day, dear?" suggested her mother.

"No, I'd like to buy it now, and then I can have it to read on Christmas Day. Do come, Mother!"

The book department was upstairs, and proved as crowded as the floor below. After some difficulty they managed to find a place at the counter, and Muriel was soon occupied in turning over the pages of various fascinating stories, hesitating so long over her choice that the ten minutes soon lengthened out into a quarter of an hour.

"Do be quick, Muriel!" Patty ventured to whisper. "Aunt Lucy wants to go home, and I haven't bought one of my presents yet!"

"Oh, bother!" replied Muriel. "Do you think you'd have this historical tale, or this school story, if you were choosing?"

"The school one," said Patty, "though either looks nice. Here's the assistant. If you buy it now, perhaps Aunt Lucy would take me to the toy department for just five minutes."

"I can't make up my mind yet," said Muriel. "I'd rather look at a few others first. Hand me that one bound in green. Yes, and the red one too. Oh, don't be a nuisance! Your Christmas presents will have to wait. I'm not going to decide in a hurry just to please you."

Poor Patty thought Muriel would never finish her purchase. She examined book after book, till at length even her mother waxed impatient, and declared she could stay no longer.

"It is twenty minutes past twelve now," she said, "and I have made an appointment at half-past to meet the superintendent of the Sunday School about the Scholars' Christmas Tree. I should not like to keep him waiting, and I am afraid I shall be late as it is. You must choose at once, dear, and come."

It took almost five minutes longer to secure the services of the assistant, who in the meantime had been attending to somebody else, and to wait while she wrapped the book in paper and fetched the change: so when at length Muriel was able to take her parcel, Mrs. Pearson was most anxious to start for home.

"I suppose there's no time for me to buy anything?" ventured Patty, timidly.

"Oh no, dear!" said her aunt. "We must hurry away at once; you should have mentioned it before. What did you want to get?"

"Some little presents for the children," said Patty. "I've brought my purse with me."

"I am sending them a parcel to-morrow," said Mrs. Pearson, "so that will do for you as well. You shall help me to pack it if you like. Dear me, it's nearly half-past twelve already! How very annoying! Jackson must drive home as quickly as he can. I shall have to apologize to Mr. Saunders. He's always so punctual, I'm sure I shall find him in the breakfast-room when we arrive."

Patty entered the carriage in a very dejected frame of mind. It seemed so hard, when the money had been in her pocket all the morning, that she should have found no opportunity of spending it. She had wished so much to send Christmas boxes to the little ones, and though she knew her aunt's gifts would probably be much handsomer than any she could have afforded, she felt it was not at all the same as if they were her own.

"It's the first Christmas I've ever been away from home," she said to herself, "and I wanted everyone to have a remembrance from me. They'll be so disappointed, and think I've taken no trouble over them. I haven't even any cards to send them."

In spite of her efforts she could not get over her disappointment, and as she sat by the breakfast-room fire after lunch, the tears began to well up in her eyes at the thought of the delightful parcel which she had hoped by now to be packing up and despatching. Muriel, seated in the opposite armchair, was absorbed in her new story, and beyond occasionally asking Patty to poke the fire or put on more coals, took no notice of her cousin, and did not see that anything was wrong. Patty tried to fix her attention on "The Daisy Chain", which she had just begun to read, but the description of the large family made her think of her own, and she felt so wretchedly homesick and miserable that big drops blurred her eyes and fell down on to the pages of her book. She was wiping them up carefully with her pocket handkerchief when the door opened suddenly, and Cousin Horace made his appearance.

"Hello!" he cried cheerily. "I thought I should find you two in here! Muriel, Mother wants you for a minute in her bedroom."

"What for?"

"Your new dress has come, I believe."

Muriel jumped up with alacrity and went upstairs, and Horace, taking her vacant chair, stretched himself lazily, and put his feet on the fender.

"I don't know what it is about holidays," he remarked; "they make a fellow want to do nothing but lounge. Don't you feel the same, Patty?"

"I'm not sure," said Patty, so very chokily that Horace sat up and examined her with critical eyes.

"Why, what's the matter?" he exclaimed.

"Nothing," said Patty, "at least, not much."

"But you're crying."

It was such a self-evident statement that Patty did not reply.

"Have you been quarrelling with Muriel?"

"No. Oh no!"

"Then what is it?"

"It seems hardly worth while telling."

"Of course it is. Look here, Patty, you and I are chums. If you've anything on your mind, just reel it off and get rid of it. Perhaps I can help."

"It's only about the children," began Patty.

"Well! Go on! What about them?"

"I meant to buy them some presents, and there was no time when we were shopping this morning, and Aunt Lucy isn't going into town again before Christmas, so I can't get them at all now," said Patty, blurting out her trouble as briefly as she could.

"Is that all?" asked Horace.

"It's quite enough for me," replied Patty, wiping her eyes again.

"Why, my dear girl, that's easily remedied. Put on your hat and jacket and I'll take you to town in the tramcar. It's only half-past three, and we'll soon buy what you want."

"Oh! Would Aunt Lucy really let us?" cried Patty, brightening up at such a delightful prospect.

"Why not? We'll go and ask her. Stuff that handkerchief in your pocket, and come along now."

Horace knew exactly the right way to wheedle his mother, and very soon persuaded her to allow them to start on their expedition.

"Patty must put on her fur," said Mrs. Pearson. "It is much too cold and foggy for Muriel to go out. I heard her coughing last night."

"I don't want to go, thanks," said Muriel, who looked a little annoyed. "Horace can please himself. I thought he said he was going to develop my films."

"I'll do that another day. Be quick, Patty, or you'll find everything bought up before you get there! I expect the shops will be crammed as full of people as they'll hold."

It was in very different spirits indeed that Patty buttoned her boots, and, donning her outdoor garments, joined Horace, who was waiting for her in the hall. It was freezing keenly, and the ground crunched crisply under their feet as they walked down the drive. They were obliged to wait nearly ten minutes for the tramcar, and it was bitterly cold standing at the corner of the road, but Patty did not mind in the least when she thought of her errand. It was almost dark before they reached the town, and the streets looked bright and cheerful, with their many gas lamps and electric lights shining out through the murky atmosphere. Everyone appeared to be busy with Christmas shopping, and the pavements were crowded with people gazing at the presents displayed in the windows: and almost all seemed to be carrying a number of parcels. There was such a happy, cheery feeling in the air, in spite of the fog, that Patty felt inclined to smile at everybody she met, even the conductor who came to collect their fares, or the stout woman who sat next to her, and whose large basket was such an inconvenience. She was beaming with joy as she and Horace left the car at the terminus and walked down the main street, looking at the gay shop windows as they went.

"I hope you've made a list of your presents," said Horace, "and then we shan't waste time. I think the best plan is to go to a shop, ask for what you want, and insist upon having it. Don't let them show you half-a-dozen other things, and try to persuade you they're quite as good."

"I haven't made a list," said Patty, "but I want to buy eight presents, and only spend three shillings. It allows just fourpence-halfpenny for each, or if I could spend a little less on some of the children's, I might afford rather more for Father's."

"Whew!" exclaimed Horace. "It requires rather careful calculation. You'll have to be uncommonly economical, I'm afraid. What can you possibly buy for fourpence-halfpenny that's worth having?"

"A great many things," said Patty. "Toys, of course, for the little ones. It's far harder to choose presents for Basil and Milly, and it will be terribly difficult to get one for Father, I'm sure. Why, there's Uncle Sidney! He's seen us, and he's crossing the street."

"Well, Patty," said Mr. Pearson, "what are you and Horace doing here?"

"We've come shopping," explained Horace. "Patty's going to hunt bargains to send home. She wants to buy eight Christmas presents for three shillings. Isn't she plucky?" he added, with a meaning glance at his father.

"You had better take her to Archer's stores," said Mr. Pearson, "and see what you can find there." Then, putting his hand in his pocket, he drew out a sovereign and slipped it into his niece's hand. "This is my present to you, Patty," he said. "Perhaps you would rather have it now than on Christmas Day. Spend it just as you like, my dear," and he hurried away almost before she had time to say "Thank you".

With such wealth at her disposal, Patty could now afford to be extravagantly generous, and I think she never enjoyed any afternoon in her life more than the one spent in Archer's stores. I fear she tried Horace's patience, after all, by looking at a great many unnecessary articles; but in the end she secured exactly what she wanted, and emerged from the crowded shop in such a state of bliss that he forbore to scold, and took her various packages instead—a great self-denial on his part, for he was a young gentleman who considered it much beneath his dignity to carry a parcel. I do not know which delighted Patty most, when she opened her treasures on her return, whether it was the pair of thick driving gloves for her father, or the books for Basil and Milly, or the wonderful toys for the little ones. Mary, the nurse, had not been forgotten—a pretty handkerchief-box was to bear her name; and there was even a bottle of scent for Anne, the kitchen servant, and a pencil-case for Hughes, the coachman.

"They'll be so surprised," she said. "I'm sure they won't expect such lovely presents as these."

"These aren't nearly so nice as the things Mother's sending them," said Muriel, turning over the toys in a rather disdainful manner.

"No, but they'll like them all the same, because they come from me. It will be so delightful to write 'From Patty' on each."

"Well, I should hardly have thought it worth while to go into town on purpose to buy them, and especially to drag poor Horace out on such a cold, foggy afternoon," said Muriel.

"She didn't drag me out, Sis; it was I who suggested it," interposed Horace. "Why can't you let her enjoy her presents without finding fault with them?"

"I'm not finding fault."

"Yes, you are."

"You're quite absurd about Patty."

"And you're not very kind."

"It's the first time you've ever called me unkind," said Muriel, flushing angrily. "I think it's horrid of you to run away from me for a whole afternoon and then speak to me like this! You're unkind yourself!"

And throwing down the humming top which she had been examining, she stalked out of the room, and banged the door behind her. Horace, who was extremely fond of his sister, followed, and succeeded in making peace. Muriel was mollified when he played chess with her all the evening, and forgave him for what she considered his neglect; but his championship of Patty did not make her love her cousin any the better.

CHAPTER IX

An Afternoon with Jean

IF Patty had to rub her eyes rather vigorously with her pocket handkerchief on Christmas morning, I think there was every excuse for her. To be in a home which was not her own home seemed in some respects almost harder than being at school, for however kind relations may prove, they can never quite take the place of one's family on such a festival as Christmas Day. There were, of course, no presents for Patty from Kirkstone, nothing but a much-disinfected letter, which Aunt Lucy viewed with great uneasiness, and insisted that her niece should throw into the fire directly she had read it.

"I have such a horror of scarlet fever," she declared. "Neither Horace nor Muriel has ever had it, and germs can certainly be conveyed through notepaper. It will be wise, I think, to burn some sulphur pastilles in the room, and you had better wash your hands, Patty, with carbolic soap, as you have touched the letter. I hope your mother won't write to you very often. It would be much safer simply to send telegrams to say how the children are getting on. I'd really rather you didn't receive postcards from Milly."

"But Milly is quite well, and doesn't go near the ones who are ill," pleaded Patty.

"She might develop the disease at any time, though," said Mrs. Pearson. "It's wiser to run no risks. I shall write to your father to-day, and mention the matter."

To lose Milly's daily postcards was a sad blow.

"I'm sure it's not necessary," thought Patty. "Father is so careful; he wouldn't let there be the slightest danger. Still, I suppose Aunt Lucy is nervous, and of course when I'm staying here I can't have letters if she's afraid of them. I do hope she'll let me go and have tea with Jean. I shall be dreadfully disappointed if she says 'No'."

Jean's invitation was the event to which Patty looked forward most during the holidays, but it was a little doubtful whether she would be allowed to accept it, as, though they did not live far away, the Bannermans were not personal friends of Mr. and Mrs. Pearson. A letter arrived one morning from Jean, addressed to Muriel, asking both the girls to tea on the following Thursday, and, to Patty's dismay, her cousin at once declared that she did not intend to go.

"Jean Bannerman's all very well at school, but I really don't want to know her during the holidays," said Muriel. "I see quite as much of her at The Priory as I want. Do you think we need accept, Mother?"

"Well, darling, I must think about it," said Mrs. Pearson. "I have never been introduced to Mrs. Bannerman, and I don't usually let you go to houses where I don't visit myself. Still, on the other hand, I shouldn't like you to disappoint your schoolfellow or hurt her feelings."

"She won't be disappointed; she doesn't care about me in the least," said Muriel.

"Then why does she ask you?"

"I'm sure I don't know," replied Muriel, who never paused to consider that the invitation was also for Patty, and to consult her wishes on the subject of accepting it.

"I hardly know what excuse we can give," said Mrs. Pearson doubtfully.

"We must give some," persisted Muriel, "because the Holdens said they were going to ask me for Thursday, and I particularly want to go there. I expect I shall hear from Trissie this evening. Can't we wait till to-morrow to answer Jean's letter?"

Muriel's expected invitation arrived the following morning, and furnished her with the excuse she needed for refusing the one from Jean.

"I shall write to her and say we can't either of us accept," she said decisively.

"Because you are both engaged for that afternoon," added Mrs. Pearson.

"Well, the Holdens haven't invited Patty," said Muriel, "but of course it doesn't matter."

"If I ask Mrs. Holden to include her in the invitation, I am sure she will do so," said Mrs. Pearson.

"If it won't make too many," began Muriel, frowning at the suggestion.

"Oh, Aunt Lucy!" cried Patty, waxing bold, "if the Holdens haven't really sent me an invitation, may I have tea with Jean instead? I should so like to go."

"It would certainly be a good way out of the difficulty," said Mrs. Pearson. "I think that will be quite the best plan. You had better write, Muriel, and say that you have an engagement yourself, but your cousin will be pleased to accept."

Patty had never expected such luck as to be able to spend a whole afternoon with Jean without Muriel accompanying her, and she found it quite difficult to repress her delight. The time fixed was three o'clock, and punctual to the moment she started off, under the escort of one of the servants, to walk to the Bannermans' house, which was only a short distance from Thorncroft. Jean was watching for her at the window, and flew to the front door to welcome her.

"Here you are at last!" she exclaimed, when her friend was safely inside the hall. "I'm simply rejoiced to have you all to myself! I was obliged to ask Muriel too, but I'm so glad she couldn't come. Now we'll have a glorious time. Come into the drawing-room to see Mother, and then we'll go upstairs to my bedroom. I have ever so many things I want to show you."

Jean was the fortunate possessor of a particularly pretty little bedroom. It was furnished partly as a sitting-room, and a fire had been lighted there that afternoon, so that the two girls might indulge in a private chat. Patty sank into a cosy basket chair, but she did not stay there long, as she kept jumping up to look at the many treasures which decorated the walls, and about most of which Jean seemed to have some story to tell. Over the mantelpiece hung a fine pair of ram's horns that had been polished and mounted on an oak slab.

"They came from Scotland," said Jean, "and they're a souvenir of an adventure that Colin and I had when we were staying at our Uncle's."

"What happened?"

"We went out one day for a walk by ourselves on the hills. We had wandered a long way, and climbed over a stone wall into a field, when suddenly we heard a curious noise, and saw an old ram stamping its feet at us. 'We'd better run,' said Colin. 'It'll be after us in a moment;' and just as he spoke, the ram set off as fast as it could in our direction. You can imagine how we rushed down the hill. The ram looked so fierce, we were dreadfully frightened, and I thought perhaps it would gore us like a bull. At the bottom of the field there was a stream. Colin called to me to get across by the stones, and I tried, but I was in such a hurry that my foot slipped, and I fell into quite a deep pool up to my waist. The ram seemed at first as if it meant to follow me, for it came a little way into the water; but it changed its mind, and turned round and went up the hill again. Colin fished me out of the water, but I was dreadfully wet, and so out of breath with running, I felt as if I couldn't walk home; so he took me to a farm close by, and the people dried my clothes. They were very kind, especially when they heard about the ram. They said it was really a savage one, and it might have hurt us if it had caught us. They were obliged to kill it that autumn, and they sent the horns to Uncle as a present; and he had them mounted, and gave them to me. When I see them hanging there, I often remember how fast Colin and I ran that day."

"I should think you have splendid times in Scotland."

"So we do. We go there nearly every summer, and stay either with Grandfather or one of our uncles. When we're at Grandfather's we have to go to church on Sunday in the boat across the loch. It's so nice, especially if we go to the evening service, and row back just at sunset. Then on weekdays we go fishing. I caught a salmon all by myself last year. I was so proud. Grandfather didn't touch my line, he only told me what to do. We took a photo. of the salmon, and I had it framed. It's there, hanging on the wall. You must look at it, and at some of my other pictures."

"I like that picture best," said Patty, smiling, and pointing to a corner where there was a little stained-glass window opening on to the landing. Against the outside of this two noses were flattened, and two pairs of eyes were plainly visible gazing into the room with deep interest, while a peculiar noise, something between giggling and snorting, seemed to indicate that the owners of the eyes and noses were making an effort to subdue their mirth.

"Nell and Jamie!" cried Jean, springing up in a hurry. "They are the most outrageous children!"

There was a loud scuffle, the sound of a falling chair and of flying footsteps, and by the time Jean reached the door no one was to be seen, though a doll, dropped in the hurried flight, afforded some evidence of the intruders.

"I suppose they wanted to peep at you," said Jean. "Mother told them they must be good this afternoon, and not bother if I wanted to have you to myself. As a rule they cling to me like burs from morning till night."

"Oh, do let us go to see them!" said Patty.

"Very well, but you don't know what you're undertaking," said Jean, leading the way to the nursery. "You won't get rid of them all the rest of the time you're here."

Nell and Jamie proved to be roguish-looking little people of seven and five, with round, pink, dimpled cheeks, and crops of beautiful thick auburn curls. They were the babies of the household, and Patty could see that Jean, though she affected to find them troublesome, was secretly immensely proud of them, and pleased to have an opportunity of showing them to her friend. They were not at all shy; both climbed readily upon the visitor's knees, and began to talk in a most friendly fashion.

"We're going to be very good," announced Jamie, whose small fingers were busy examining Patty's brooch and locket. "We're not going to do anything we oughtn't."

"So you say," said Jean, "but you haven't asked Patty if she likes her locket opened. Be careful, Jamie! You'll break the hinge if you bend it back. Don't let him, Patty! Put him down if he's a nuisance."

"I like to nurse him," said Patty. "He reminds me of my little brother Rowley. I think I'll take off the locket and put it in my pocket, and then it can't come to any harm. What a heavy boy you are, Jamie, for your age! I'm sure you weigh as much as Nell."

"'Cause I eat more," said Jamie. "I can always win when we have bread and butter races at tea. How do you like my new blouse? Nurse only finished it half an hour ago. She made it on purpose because you were coming. She said I had nothing else to put on."

"Oh, Jamie, I'm sure she didn't!" exclaimed Jean. "You have a whole drawer full of clean blouses."

"They're all dirty now, every one," confided Nell. "He had on five yesterday, and two this morning. He spilt his porridge down one at breakfast, and he nursed Floss in the other. She had just come in from the garden, and her paws were so muddy."

"I'm afraid he's a handful!" said Patty, kissing the pretty little fellow who clung round her neck in such a coaxing manner.

"He certainly is," said Jean. "What do you think he did last Sunday? He had promised to be extra good in church, and he was so quiet, we thought he was behaving beautifully, and then I looked, and found he was rubbing his face along the hot-water pipes, and had made black smears all across his cheeks, and on his white sailor collar. He's an extremely naughty boy sometimes, I can assure you. Nell, I wish you'd go and find Colin. He wants to see you, Patty, very much; but he's so dreadfully shy with girls, I don't know whether we shall be able to persuade him to come into the room after all."

Nell returned in a few minutes, hauling the bashful and unwilling Colin by the hand. He was a boy of thirteen, like Jean in appearance, and rather gruff and abrupt in his manners, until he found that Patty was not so formidable as he had imagined, and that she had a brother the same age as himself, who had also won a prize for the long jump at his school sports.

"Colin's still at a preparatory," explained Jean, "but he's to go to a public school next year, either Marlborough or Rugby—Father can't quite decide which."

"Which would you rather?" enquired Patty.

"Rugby, because a fellow I know is there," replied Colin, decisively.

"I shall go to Rugby too, when Colin does," announced Jamie confidently.

"No, thanks! I wouldn't take you with those curls. You may go to The Priory with Jean," said Colin teasingly.

"Would you take me without my curls?"

"They'd certainly have to shear you first."

"Then I'll cut them off now, my own self!" cried Jamie, jumping from Patty's knee and rummaging in his nurse's workbasket for her scissors, which his sister promptly took away from him.

"Look here, Curlylocks!" she said. "If you cut your hair you won't get any more chocolates. No, not a single one ever again. I should give them all to Nell to eat instead. It's quite true. I mean it. I do indeed."

"I don't want to go to school yet," declared Nell. "Jean says you have to sit so still in class, and not even whisper. Miss Thornton tells me to run six times round the room when I begin to get tired."

"I'm afraid Miss Harper wouldn't let us do that, however much we might fidget," laughed Patty. "I should like to see her face if we suggested it. Is Miss Thornton your governess?"

"Yes; she comes every morning, but we're having holidays now. I like holidays best."

"So do most people," said Jean; "but it's not much of a holiday for anybody to sit nursing two big children. Come along, Patty! I want Colin to show you his birds' eggs. He's got quite a nice collection."

"Us too!" cried the little ones, holding out beseeching hands. "We won't touch a thing."

Colin, however, was firm in his refusal.

"No, thank you," he said. "I'd as soon let Floss loose among my birds' eggs as trust you two."

"But we'd promise."

"I don't believe your promises. You'd break them in three seconds, and the eggs as well. You smashed all those I gave you last term. Here, you may have this blue chalk pencil and draw pictures. Don't quarrel over it more than you can help."

The collection of birds' eggs was kept downstairs, so, leaving Nell and Jamie in the nursery, the girls went with Colin to the breakfast-room, where there were Jean's foreign stamps to look at afterwards, and a large album full of picture postcards. Mr. Bannerman came in for tea, and was so pleasant and jovial and full of fun, that he entertained them all for more than half an hour with his jokes and stories. He had travelled much in his youth, and had many tales to tell of wild adventures in far-off countries, or amusing experiences nearer home. He joined afterwards in playing games, in which the little ones were also included; and the time passed away so quickly, that Patty could scarcely believe it was eight o'clock when Aunt Lucy's maid arrived to fetch her home.

"I expect you had a stupid afternoon," said Muriel, on her return, "one of those tiresome duty visits that have to be paid now and then, worse luck!"

"On the contrary, I enjoyed it immensely," said Patty.

"Why, what did you do? I can't imagine there'd be anything exciting at the Bannermans'."

"Oh! we played games, and looked at birds' eggs, and postcards, and things."

"That doesn't sound interesting in the least. You should have been at the Holdens'. They have a pianola and a gramophone, and we were trying over all the new pantomime songs."

"I liked being with Jean."

"I don't know what you see in Jean. I think she's a most stupid, commonplace girl. I'm not at all anxious to be friends with her in Waverton, and I'm very glad I couldn't go to-day. You were welcome to my share of the visit if you enjoyed it, but please don't suggest to Mother to invite her back, because we haven't an afternoon free, and I'd rather not ask her if we had!"

CHAPTER X

The Cæsar Translation

PATTY heaved a sigh of relief when she found herself back again at school. With the exception of the one afternoon at Jean Bannerman's, she had not enjoyed her holidays. A month spent in Muriel's society had been of little pleasure; indeed, almost every day it had needed constant effort to keep her temper, and to submit patiently to her cousin's whims. Muriel, taking advantage of Patty's forbearance, had ordered her companion about, and treated her in such a haughty and disdainful manner, that the latter had sometimes felt her position nearly unbearable. At The Priory at least she could be independent; she could select her own friends, with whom she might mix on equal terms, and could secure a standing of her own, apart from Muriel's scornful patronage. It was delightful to once more meet Enid, Avis, and Winnie, and to make plans for various cherished schemes to be carried out during the term; even May, Ella, and Doris proved more friendly, and chatted quite pleasantly with her in their bedroom about their experiences: while Cissie Gardiner and Maggie Woodhall greeted her with enthusiasm.

"I've had such a lovely time!" said Cissie. "My brother Cyril was home from Sandhurst, and he took me to the Military Tournament. I think there's nothing in the world equal to cavalry. I mean to be an army sister when I grow up. We saw a staff of nurses do field drill, and carry a wounded officer to a Red Cross tent. (He wasn't really wounded, of course, but he pretended to be.) They looked just too sweet in their uniforms. Grey always suits me, doesn't it? I wish there'd be another war in South Africa, so that I might volunteer to go out."

"You won't be grown up for four years, dearest, and then perhaps you'll be tired of soldiers, and like poets again," said Maggie, putting her arm affectionately round her friend's waist. "Did you have nice holidays too, Patty?"

"Yes, thank you," replied Patty, as truthfully as she could.

She had decided that it was wiser not to tell any of her friends how unhappy she had been at Thorncroft. For Uncle Sidney's sake she would be as loyal as she could to Muriel, so, suppressing all mention of the many disagreeable episodes of her visit, she merely described the parties and the afternoon at the pantomime with as much detail as possible, leaving it to be inferred that she had enjoyed herself. The spring term was generally regarded at The Priory as a time of particularly close study and increased work. In the autumn there were lectures, concerts, or other little dissipations to break the monotony of school life; the summer term was arranged specially to allow extra time out-of-doors; but from January to April the girls were expected to put their shoulders to the wheel, and commit to memory such a number of pages in their textbooks, that Avis declared it amounted to hard labour.

"The worst of it is," she complained, "that each teacher expects you to give all your time to her particular subject. Miss Harper looks reproachful if I can't say my history, and Miss Rowe scolds if I miss in my grammar. Then Mademoiselle gives me yards of French poetry and two or three irregular verbs to learn, and Miss Lincoln asks me why my essay is so short. I could spend the whole of prep. over just one lesson, and then not know it properly in the end. Unless I take my books to bed, I can't possibly get through everything that's set me."

"You should do as I do," said Enid. "I learn the beginning of the history portion almost by heart. Then I look very intelligent and attentive, and when Miss Harper asks me a question, I rattle off a long answer nearly word for word from the book, at such a tremendous rate that she can scarcely follow me, and says, 'That will do, Enid'. It makes her think I know the whole lesson, and she keeps questioning the other girls who've hesitated and stumbled."

"She'll catch you some day," said Winnie. "Miss Harper's too clever to be taken in by any such tricks. She's sure to ask you a question at the end quite unexpectedly, and what will you do then?"

"Trust to luck," said Enid. "She'll perhaps think I've forgotten for once. I manage my essays for Miss Lincoln rather well, too. When I can't remember any facts I make up a line or two of appropriate poetry, and put 'as the poet says'. It fills up splendidly. Miss Lincoln said once she didn't recognize all my quotations, but she always gives me a high mark!"

"You can't do that kind of thing with Mademoiselle," said Avis.

"No, I own it would be no use to try. When one has forty lines of French poetry to recite, one's obliged to set to work and get it into one's head. But I mean to manage better in the conversation class. My eldest sister has just come home from Paris, and she's taught me the French for 'How is your throat?' and 'Do you feel a draught?' Mademoiselle always has a cold, and wants the window shut. She'll think I'm so sympathetic, and be sure to put 'excellent' in my report."

"I can manage French, and do pretty well in history and geography, but I can't learn Latin," groaned Winnie. "I didn't mind so much when we only did sentences, but now we've begun Cæsar it's simply detestable. I'm an absolute goose at translation."

"So am I," echoed Avis, mournfully. "I don't think Latin was ever meant for girls. My brother did Cæsar two years ago, and he's in Virgil now, though he's a year younger than I am. It seems quite easy to him, but I never know which verb goes with which substantive, or whether a thing is a nominative or a genitive. I look out all the words in the dictionary, and learn their meanings, but I can't make the least sense of them until Miss Harper shows me how they fit into the sentences. Why isn't Latin arranged like English? Everything seems turned the wrong way."

"I don't know," said Winnie. "I should think it must have been difficult for a Roman baby to learn to talk. Miss Harper says it's good mental exercise for us, and we must try to use our brains."

"Mine will wear out," said Avis. "They never were very strong, to begin with. I always forget everything I have learnt the term before; I do indeed. I knew the whole of 'Lycidas' by heart last year, and I can't remember a line of it now. Miss Rowe says my head is like a sieve. You ought to like Cæsar, at any rate, Cissie, because it's all about soldiers."

"I don't care for Roman soldiers," said Cissie; "at least, not in Cæsar, though I rather like them in stories. I love the one in *Puck of Pook's Hill*, who had to set out for the great wall; he was a perfect dear. If Rudyard Kipling could have written that wretched *De Bello Gallico* it would have been so different, and so much nicer."

"I should think it would!" said Enid laughing. "Much too nice for us. They choose the driest books possible for schools. Patty, why don't you grumble too? It's quite aggravating to see you looking so complacent."

"I grumble over mathematics, at any rate," said Patty.

"But not over Latin?"

"No, I rather like it."

"How can you like it?"

"I don't know why, but I do."

"There's nothing to like."

"Yes, there is; it's rather fun to try and turn the words into sentences."

"You're not very good at French translation, and yet you always make sense out of Cæsar. I can't think how you manage it," said Avis.

"Ah, that's my secret!" answered Patty. "I shan't give it away, or else perhaps you'd all do as well."

"Is it really a secret?" asked Beatrice Wynne, who had joined the group.

"Of course it is," said Patty mysteriously. "One of those things you can't explain and wouldn't if you could."

"Oh, do tell me!" implored Beatrice.

"No!" said Patty, shaking her head solemnly. "A secret is a secret, and you mustn't ask questions."

"I'll find out some day," returned Beatrice. "I love discovering secrets."

"Don't be too sure of mine," said Patty. "You won't find it out, because ———"

But here she shook her head with the air of a sphinx, and, leaving her sentence unfinished, took up her music-case and went to practise.

Now, Patty had only been having a little fun with Beatrice. She had meant to say, "because there is no secret at all", and to have explained what was really the fact, that she had helped her brother Basil so often at home to prepare his Latin translation that the earlier part of *De Bello Gallico* was already familiar to her. Thinking, however, that it would be possible to continue the joke, and that it would be amusing to excite Beatrice's curiosity over nothing, she had preserved her mystery for the present, intending to explain it on some future occasion. In view of events which followed, it proved a most unfortunate occurrence, and one which she afterwards bitterly regretted. Her innocent remark led to conclusions quite unforeseen, and so disastrous that she would have given much if her words had never been uttered; but once spoken they were impossible to recall, and the mischief was done. Blind as yet to what was to happen in the future, she spent half an hour at the piano, and then went to the classroom to fetch a book which she had forgotten. It was a pouring wet afternoon, and as it was quite impossible for the girls to play their usual game of hockey, they were allowed to amuse themselves as they liked until tea-time. As a rule the classroom was empty between three and four o'clock, and Patty opened the door, expecting to find the room unoccupied. To her astonishment, Muriel was seated there, busily engaged in writing, and evidently copying something from a book which she held on her knee. She started guiltily at her cousin's entrance, as if she were being caught in some act which she did not wish to be discovered, turned crimson, and, thrusting the book into her desk, banged down the lid, and pretended to be tidying the contents of her pencil-box. It was so unusual to find Muriel at work out of school hours, that Patty could not help expressing her amazement.

"Why, what are you doing here?" she exclaimed.

"I might ask you the same," returned Muriel. "I suppose I have as good a right to come to my desk when I want as anybody else has!"

"Why, of course," said Patty. "I was only surprised."

"Then I wish you would keep your surprise to yourself. I can't think why you should always be following me about."

"Oh, Muriel, I wasn't! I only came to fetch my history."

"And I only came to do some of my lessons in quiet. The recreation room is a perfect Babel."

"So it is," said Patty. "I thought I'd learn my dates quietly in here."

"Can't you learn them in prep.?" asked Muriel.

"Not so well. I want the extra time for my Latin. It's such a stiff piece for to-morrow. Don't you think so?"

"I haven't looked at it yet," replied Muriel, in a rather strained voice, and avoiding Patty's eye.

"Why, Muriel," cried the latter, who had come close to her cousin, "what are you writing now? 'There remained one way through the Sequani.'"

"I wish you'd mind your own business. I was only scribbling nonsense to try my new pen," said Muriel angrily, tearing up her piece of paper. "Do leave me alone!"

Patty sat down at her own desk, and, taking out her history book, was soon deep in an effort to master the dates which Miss Harper had set for the next day's lesson. Muriel went on for some little time arranging her pencils and indiarubbers in a very discontented and annoyed manner.

"Look here, Patty, I wish you'd go!" she said at last.

"Go! Why?" asked Patty.

"Because you disturb me."

"But I wasn't saying it aloud."

"It doesn't matter. I can learn things much better when I'm quite alone."

"You're never alone at prep."

"No, I wish I were. I could get through the work in half the time. You're interrupting me now by talking."

"Then I won't talk," said Patty, taking up her book, which she had laid down; "I won't say a single word."

"The very sight of anyone in the room is enough to stop me learning properly. I haven't done a single thing since you came here."

Patty was on the point of saying, "It's your own fault, then;" but the thought of Uncle Sidney stepped in, and she refrained.

"What do you want me to do?" she asked instead.

"To go and leave me in peace. You can learn your dates in a corner of the lecture room or in the studio."

It was rather hard to be thus ordered away from the quiet place which she had chosen, and Patty stood hesitating whether to comply or not, when the question was settled by the ringing of the tea bell, and both girls were obliged to hurry to the refectory. Patty did not think much of this incident at the time, only setting it down to Muriel's caprice, and being quite accustomed to her cousin's ill humours; but in the light of after events it wore a different aspect. One morning at nine o'clock, when Miss Rowe had taken the register, and the girls were in their places waiting for school to begin, Miss Harper entered the room with an extremely grave look on her face. Instead of commencing the lesson as usual, she stood for a few moments without speaking, and her silence filled her class with an uneasy apprehension that all was not right.

"Girls," she said at last, "something has happened which gives me more pain than anything else I have experienced during the five years I have taught at The Priory. Yesterday the monitress, when tidying the room, found this book, which she very rightly brought at once to me. I regret to tell you that it is a translation of Cæsar's *De Bello Gallico*; in fact, what is commonly known as a 'crib'. That any girl in my class could so have lost her self-respect as to condescend to use it to prepare her lesson, fills me with shame, as it shows such an absolute lowering of the high standard of honour which we have always tried to maintain. I ask each of you now, do you know who is the owner of this book, or can you account for its presence here?"

There was no reply. Every girl looked at her neighbour, but nobody had any information to volunteer. Muriel's eyes were fixed on her atlas; she did not appear the least affected by Miss Harper's words, though a keen observer might have noticed she was a little paler than usual. Patty's heart beat quickly. Quite suddenly the horrible remembrance flashed across her of the book which Muriel had replaced so quickly in the desk. Muriel had certainly at the time been writing a translation of the Latin lesson, though she had denied it flatly; and it was a curious coincidence that she should have seemed so unreasonably angry with her cousin for staying in the room. Was the book hers? Patty blushed hotly at the very idea. What ought she to do? It was impossible to tell her conjectures to Miss Harper in the presence of the whole class. If Muriel were guilty, she would surely confess the matter herself. It could not be necessary to turn informer and voice suspicions which, after all, might prove to have been entirely groundless. Nevertheless, she felt uncomfortable, and as Miss Harper's steady glance was fixed upon her she could not meet the searching eyes, and dropped her own uneasily.

"I ask you again," said the teacher, with reproach in her voice, "does any girl know anything of this occurrence? I promise I will inflict no punishment if whoever is guilty will only honestly confess."

Once more her brown eyes scanned her class narrowly, and once more Patty dared not look her straight in the face.

"Very well," said Miss Harper, "I shall not seek any further to find the owner, though the initials P. and H. intertwined on the title page might possibly give me a clue. The girl to whom it belongs will find her own conscience her severest judge; she will surely feel, without further remark from me, how contemptible is her conduct. I scarcely know what to do with this book," she continued, holding up the translation as if she did not like to touch it. "I will not take charge of it, as I consider it unworthy to be in existence. This will show you best how I regard it;" and, tearing its pages across and across, she flung it into the fire. "Now, girls, open your Cæsars, and we will begin the lesson."

"GIRLS," SHE CRIED, "SURELY YOU CAN'T SUSPECT ME OF OWNING THAT WRETCHED CRIB"

It was the most miserable Latin class which the girls ever remembered. Each one was afraid to construe well, for fear she might be suspected of having done her preparation with the aid of the translation. Miss Harper made no comments, and gave neither praise for good work nor blame for bad. She took the marks as usual, and at the end of the hour left the room without referring again to the subject. I am afraid Miss Rowe, who followed with geology, did not find her pupils particularly intelligent that morning. She was obliged several times to correct them sharply for wandering attention, and was annoyed at the many wrong answers to the questions which she asked. The girls were unable to fix their thoughts upon either glaciers or moraines; all were counting the minutes until lunch-time, when they could rush from the room to discuss the burning question of the ownership of the translation. As Patty walked down the passage at eleven o'clock to the pantry, she noticed Vera Clifford nudge Kitty Harrison and whisper something she could not hear. Most of the girls were collected in a little group near the door, talking eagerly, and some of them looked curiously at her as she passed.

"I don't believe it!" cried Enid's indignant voice. "It's quite untrue and impossible!"

"You'll never persuade me, not if you try all day," said Winnie.

"She always gets such good marks for her Cæsar," said Maggie Woodhall, doubtfully.

"Well, she told me herself it was a secret how she did it," declared Beatrice Wynne. "She said she couldn't explain it, and wouldn't if she could, and if we knew we might all do it equally well. Could anything be clearer than that?"

"And the initials were P. H., for Patty Hirst!" added Ella Johnson.

Patty, as she took her lunch, could not help overhearing what was said by the group round the door. At first she did not quite understand the drift of the conversation, but at Ella's remark a light suddenly dawned upon her. Putting down her glass of milk, she turned abruptly to the others.

"Girls," she cried, "surely you can't suspect me of owning that wretched 'crib'?"

"Then whose is it if it's not yours?" asked Beatrice Wynne.

"I don't know, any more than you. But one thing's certain, I've had nothing to do with it. Why, I wouldn't have soiled my fingers by touching it!"

"How about the initials?" enquired Ella Johnson, with a touch of sarcasm in her voice.

"I don't know. It never occurred to me till this minute that you could connect my name with them."

"It's a funny coincidence," sneered Vera Clifford.

"I suppose the book must have been brought to school by somebody," said Kitty Harrison.

"It was not brought by me," said Patty. "I've no means of proving anything, but I've always been called truthful at home, and I think my word ought to hold good at The Priory too."

"Then whom does it belong to?" persisted Kitty. "Do you know anything at all about it?"

"Nothing," answered Patty; but the horrible suspicion lurking in the corner of her mind made her voice falter just a little, and some of the girls drew their own conclusions.

"Look here," said Enid, "I'd as soon believe Miss Harper smuggled that 'crib' into school herself as think Patty did! She's absolutely incapable of such a thing, and you all know it as well as I do. Why, it's Patty who's always tried to make us be fair over our work! She simply couldn't cheat. Hands up, all those who don't believe this hateful story!"

Jean, Winnie, and Avis held up their hands at once, and so, to the astonishment of most of her companions, did Muriel. Cissie Gardiner and Maggie Woodhall followed suit, but the others looked doubtful.

"I suppose we must accept Patty's word," said Beatrice, rather stiffly. "Still, it's a funny thing, and I wish it hadn't happened."

"Very funny, certainly, for the one who started the pledge," said Vera Clifford, under her breath.

"We shall find it out some day," said Enid. "I'm determined Patty's name shall be cleared. How any of you can be so idiotic as to connect her with it, I can't imagine. Never mind, Patty dear! We know you better than to believe such rubbish. Don't trouble your head about it, for it simply isn't worth worrying over. Everyone with a spark of sense will agree with me, and I'm sure Miss Harper will think the same."

CHAPTER XI

The Summer Term

In spite of Enid's advice not to worry about the Cæsar translation, Patty could not help taking the matter deeply to heart. Though none of the girls openly accused her, she felt that the unjust suspicion clung to her, and that many were undecided whether to consider her guilty or innocent. That she, of all in the class, the one who had striven so hard for the cause of right and honour, should be obliged to remain with this blot upon the white page of her school career, seemed the greatest trial which she could be called upon to bear. The worst of it was that she could not even discuss it freely with her friends. The more she thought about the affair, the more sure she felt that the book must have belonged to Muriel, and the latter's rather conscious manner only confirmed her suspicion. The class, finding that Muriel disliked to hear the subject mentioned, naturally concluded that she was ashamed for her cousin's name to be connected with anything dishonourable, and by common consent never alluded to it in her presence. Muriel avoided Patty more than ever, confining herself strictly to Vera Clifford's company, and keeping aloof from the rest of the girls, who, indeed, found her so supercilious and disagreeable that they were not very anxious to be on friendly terms with her. Miss Harper, since burning the translation, had not referred to it again; yet, though she did not apparently relax any of the trust which she usually placed in her pupils, all were conscious of an increased vigilance in her observation of them.

"She's watching us," said Avis one day. "I can't quite describe how, but I feel as if Miss Harper knew all that I was doing and saying, and even thinking. I believe her eyes and ears must be sharper than anybody else's. She seems to notice such tiny little things, and then speaks of them quite a long time afterwards. She remembered perfectly well, I'm sure, that it was Beatrice Wynne who used always to borrow other people's pencils last term and never give them back, because when Beatrice lent her one yesterday she said so pointedly that she should return it."

It was impossible to tell from the teacher's manner whether she considered the translation had really belonged to Patty. Her remark at the time about the initials certainly favoured such a supposition, but she made no difference in her behaviour, and, indeed, several times praised Patty's work during the Latin lesson. The ownership of the book seemed likely to remain an unsolved mystery, one of those unpleasant occurrences which happen sometimes in a school, to the grief of the mistresses and the consternation of all concerned. The only thing which it was possible for Patty to do was to live the affair down, and trust that time and patient waiting might one day re-establish her reputation absolutely and beyond a doubt in the opinion of both teachers and comrades. The remainder of the spring term passed without any special event, and by Easter Mrs. Hirst wrote to say that the children were now in the best of health, that scarlet-fever germs had long ago been disinfected away, and that all the family were looking forward eagerly to her return. Patty thought there never had been such a meeting, or such glorious holidays as followed afterwards. It was almost worth while to have been absent for seven whole months to experience the joy of such a warm welcome as she found waiting for her at home. The little ones clung to her like flies round a honey pot, and even the baby, grown out of all knowledge, soon made friends with the sister whom he had forgotten. She had several delightful drives with her father when he went on his rounds, and in the long chats with her mother, after the younger ones were in bed, she was able to pour out most of her troubles, and get that comfort and good counsel which mothers always seem to know best how to give.

"I wish Muriel would like me better!" confided Patty. "It seems no use; however hard I try to be nice to her, everything I do is always wrong. Am I really keeping my promise to Uncle Sidney, when she never gives me the chance to be her friend?"

"Certainly, if you are trying your best," said Mrs. Hirst. "We cannot force our friendship where it is not wanted. You can await your opportunity of doing Muriel a good turn; some day she may appreciate you better. Kindness is never wasted, and even if it does not seem to have any immediate result, it is doing its own quiet work, and may return to you afterwards in ways which you never expect. We rarely find people exactly to our liking, so the best plan is to pick out their good points, and ignore the disagreeable side as much as we can. One of the greatest secrets in life is to know how to smile and wait. I am sure you will never regret being patient with Muriel, and who can tell that she may not change her views, and learn to value what she now throws away."

Patty went back to school much consoled, and in a far more cheerful frame of mind. She was determined that she would not let Muriel's unkindness distress her any more. She would not avoid her cousin, but, on the other hand, she would not make advances which would lay her open to a rebuff, or give any opportunity for that scornful treatment which had hurt her so much in the past. As her mother suggested, she would be ready to help if occasion offered, but there seemed no need to press services which were evidently neither desired nor welcome. Having settled that point with her own conscience, Patty began thoroughly to enjoy the summer term. The Priory was delightfully situated in the midst of pretty country, and the girls were allowed many rambles in the woods or on the heathery common. Occasionally the botany class would make an excursion, under the superintendence of Miss Rowe, to obtain specimens of wild flowers, which they afterwards pressed and pasted in books; and once Miss Lincoln took the whole of the lower school to hunt for fossils among the heaps of shale lying at the mouth of an old quarry. She herself was both a keen geologist and naturalist, and tried to interest her girls in all the specimens of stones, flowers, birds, or insects which they found during their walks. "If you will only learn to talk about things instead of people," she said, "you will avoid a great deal of disagreeable gossip and ill-natured conversation. The wide world is full of beautiful objects, and the more you know about them the less concern you will take over your neighbours' doings and failings. Real culture consists largely in being able to discuss things instead of persons. If you will lay up plenty of interests while you are young, you will find you have been like bees gathering honey, and you will have a store to draw upon for the rest of your lives quite independent of all outside happenings, or good or bad fortune which may come to you."

It was not every day, of course, that the girls could be taken for long country walks; there were many other occupations at The Priory which were quite as delightful. During the summer term the callisthenic class was given up, and swimming was held instead in the large bath beyond the gymnasium. Patty, who had not yet had any opportunity of learning to swim, looked forward with great eagerness to her first dip. The bath was very nicely arranged, with a broad walk round it, where onlookers could stand and watch, a row of small dressing-rooms at each side, and a platform at the deep end, from which diving might be performed. Patty found that she and Jean Bannerman were the only ones in the class who had not already had some practice in the water. The two beginners donned their costumes and made their initial plunge together, therefore, at the shallow end. They would have been quite content to splash about like ducks, watching the more advanced members, who were floating and swimming as if in their natural element; that, however, Miss Latimer would not allow. Placing a lifebuoy round Patty's waist, she decreed that she must commence to learn her strokes, and showed her carefully how these ought to be done. There was a long plank across the bath upon which the teacher could stand, and by means of a rope attached to the lifebuoy, could hold up her pupil until she had mastered the art of keeping herself afloat. Patty found it a great deal more difficult than she had at first imagined. She floundered and struggled helplessly in her efforts to carry out Miss Latimer's directions, foolishly opened her mouth in the water, spluttered, choked, and was very glad to take a rest, and allow Jean to have a turn instead. The latter, who had bathed often at the seaside, got on much better, and was able to inspire Patty with confidence for fresh efforts when she plucked up her courage to try again.

"You needn't be in the least afraid," said Miss Latimer encouragingly. "Everyone finds it hard at first, just like learning to ride a bicycle, or to skate, or any other unaccustomed mode of locomotion. You will soon get used to the movements, and then you will never forget them all your life; it will be as easy and natural to you as walking."

"I wish I'd got to that stage," said Patty. "Just at present I feel like one of those toy tin floating ducks that has lost its tail, and over-balances when you put it into the water. I can't remember that I ought to use both my arms and my legs. How well you managed, Jean!"

"I was practising on my bed this morning," said Jean. "Cissie and Maggie showed me the strokes. It's really rather like what a frog does, isn't it?"

"Come along; I can't waste time," said Miss Latimer. "I can give you each one more turn with the lifebuoy, and then I shall expect you to hold one another up, and try by yourselves."

By the third lesson Patty had improved so much that she was able to manage without assistance, and Miss Latimer declared that she must swim the entire length of the bath alone, from the steps to the deep end. All the class stopped floating and diving, and sat down on the edge to watch her, so that it was somewhat of an ordeal to have to perform her feat before a row of laughing eyes. She did very nicely, indeed, in the shallow part, where she could put a surreptitious foot to the bottom; but when it came to the middle, and all had to depend upon her aquatic skill, she grew nervous.

"Go on, Patty, you're all right!" called Enid.

"Throw your neck back!" cried Miss Latimer.

"Go on, Patty, keep it up!"

"Don't be done, Patty!"

"She's going under!"

"No, she's not!"

"Keep at it, Patty!"

"Don't be afraid!"

"You'll get across all right!"

In spite of her companions' encouraging remarks, however, Patty did not succeed this time. I suppose she forgot to keep her neck thrown back, or to draw in her breath properly; at any rate, up went her heels, and down went her head, and she seemed suddenly to turn a kind of somersault in the water. Instantly all the members of the class dived to her rescue, so bent on putting into performance the life-saving which they had practised, that they almost pulled her to pieces in their efforts.

"Oh, you've nearly dragged my arms off!" cried poor Patty, when at last she was in safety at the shallow end again.

"You might have been drowned if it hadn't been for us!" exclaimed Cissie Gardiner, hysterically.

"Hardly that, while I was standing by," remarked Miss Latimer, with a smile. "But Patty has given you such good practice in rescuing a drowning person, that you ought to be quite grateful to her."

"Oh, Patty, you did look funny! You came up spouting like a whale!" said Enid.

"I didn't feel funny," returned Patty. "It was horrid. I thought I was swallowing half the water in the bath."

"You won't want any tea, then!" declared Winnie.

"Yes, I shall."

"Patty must try again another day," said Miss Latimer. "She will soon gain a little more confidence, and I expect after a few weeks she will be diving at the deep end as readily as any of you. We will take the life-saving again now, with Enid to play the part of a drowning person. I was not at all satisfied with the way you pulled Patty out of the water. If such an accident had happened in a river, or in the open sea, I am afraid some of you would have been in danger yourselves."

Miss Latimer proved a true prophet, and Patty found that long before the summer term was over she was able to both dive and float, as well as swim easily round the bath. She was delighted with her new accomplishment, and began to plan already whether it would be possible to persuade her father to leave his patients and take his family to the seaside for a few weeks during the holidays, so that she might have the satisfaction of teaching the little ones what she had learnt herself.

"If he really can't spare the time," she confided to Enid, "there's a big pond at the end of a pasture near a farm, about a mile from our house. I'm sure it would be quite safe, and we could all bathe there, even Kitty and Rowley. I could float a plank on the water to hold them up while they're learning their strokes, or perhaps Mother's air cushion would be of some use, if she'd lend it to us. Basil can swim already—he learnt in the river near his school—so he'd come and help, and I'm sure they'd all enjoy it immensely, even if they only splashed about and did nothing else."

The two great recreations of the summer term at The Priory were tennis and cricket. A few girls indulged occasionally in croquet and archery, but that was only in spare time, and during the couple of hours devoted daily to outdoor exercise everybody was expected to take part in one or other of the principal games.

"You'd better choose definitely which you mean to go in for, Patty," said Winnie, "and then stick to it. If you've any aspirations towards being a tennis champion, I should advise you to keep to the courts, and practise every minute you can; but if, on the other hand, you like cricket better, I shouldn't bother with tennis if I were you."

"Winnie's right; you can't serve two masters," said Enid. "It will take your whole time if you want to do anything at tennis. The Chambers are all so splendid at it, it needs a good player to have any chance against them."

"But Miss Latimer's very hard to satisfy at cricket," said Winnie.

"So she is. She certainly doesn't allow any slack practice."

"She pegged my right leg down once to prevent my moving it, and she's most severe on a crooked bat," said Avis.

"She recollects everybody's average scores for whole years back," said Winnie. "I can't think how anybody can have such a memory."

"Miss Lincoln's the funniest," said Cissie Gardiner. "When I lost a wicket last Wednesday, she said: 'That must be because you got a bad mark for Euclid, my dear!' As if mathematics had anything to do with cricket."

Winnie laughed.

"Miss Lincoln always says: 'Those who do well in school will be equally successful in athletics'; but it's just a pleasant little fiction, like nurses telling you if you eat crusts it will make your hair curl, and it never did, because I used to finish even the hardest and most burnt ones, and my hair's as straight as a yard measure, while my little brother, who leaves all his, has a regular mop of close ringlets."

"Which do you play, Avis?" asked Patty.

"Tennis. I'm no good at all at cricket. I miss the easiest catches, and get the ball tangled in my skirts. I used to play with my brothers at home, but they always called me 'butterfingers'; so I've quite given it up, and I won't even field for them now. They tell me girls are no good at cricket."

"They should see Dora Stephenson," said Enid. "She plays as good a game as any boy, I'm sure. Miss Latimer's tremendously proud of her batting."

"Yes, I often wish I could take her home to have a match against the boys," replied Avis. "How astonished they would be! I think our old gardener would have a fit. He doesn't at all approve of girls' cricket, and told me once that 'young misses weren't meant to be lads', and I should 'only make a bad job of it'. He rolls the tennis court most beautifully, though, when he knows I'm coming back for the holidays."

"Which are you going to choose, then, Patty, cricket or tennis?" asked Enid, going back to the original subject of the conversation.

"I won't decide until I've had a good turn at each, and see which I can manage best," said Patty, diplomatically.

"All right! There's to be a match on Saturday, and I'll ask Miss Latimer to let you be in it. It's a scratch team from the Lower School against prefects and monitresses. I've no doubt we shall be badly beaten, but it really doesn't matter. It's only for practice."

"Do the prefects play well?"

"I should think so! They're very keen on it. Dora Stephenson reads up Ranjitsinhji, and Meta Hall goes to all the county matches when she can get the chance. You'll have to play up, Patty, if we want to make any score at all."

"Don't expect too much," said Patty. "I might send a catch first thing. I've played at home with Basil, but I don't know how I shall get on here."

At Enid's special request, Miss Latimer included Patty in the scratch team for the following Saturday afternoon, so that she might be able to show her capabilities and give her companions an opportunity of judging whether she might be considered fit for a place in the Lower School eleven. The prefects went in first, and the mistress, who had a keen eye for the future possibilities of her pupils, noticed with approval that Patty was not fielding like a novice, that she caught her ball neatly in her hands, instead of stopping it with her skirts, and threw it up promptly with an accuracy of aim not always common among girl players. Wishing to test her further, Miss Latimer called to her at the next over, and told her to take her turn at bowling. It was Dora Stephenson's innings, and the Lower School knew that a struggle was in store. Dora's record scores were well known, and it often seemed almost impossible to put her out. Patty walked up, quaking at the prospect of her encounter.

"Oh, Miss Latimer!" said Beatrice Wynne. "Are you sending in Patty to bowl now? It's rather hard on our side, isn't it?"

"I know what I am about, Beatrice," replied the teacher. "Go on, Patty, and don't be nervous. Let us all see what you can do."

Patty's first ball showed a science that made her companions open their eyes wide. It was a curious way of bowling, half under, half over arm, such as none of the girls had seen before, and which seemed to prove most baffling. For three balls Dora merely slogged; the fourth, to her extreme surprise, got her out.

"A duck! A duck!" cried the opposite side, in raptures of delight. To have taken her wicket in the first "over" was a success such as they had never expected, and a triumph for the Lower School not to be forgotten in a hurry.

"It was well bowled, certainly," said Dora, meeting her defeat with dignity. "I didn't think Patty could have done it. Oh, I don't grudge you a wicket! I'm only too glad to see good play, I assure you, for the credit of the school."

"It was nothing but luck, I believe," said Patty, when her friends crowded round to rejoice over her. "I daresay I couldn't do it again."

"Yes, you could," declared Enid. "It was that peculiar twist that bowled her. You'll have to teach it to us. Where did you learn it?"

"An uncle from Australia stayed with us last summer, and he showed us. Basil and I used to practise it every evening. Basil can do it far better than I can."

"You do it quite well enough. You've made your reputation this afternoon, and you're sure to be put in the Lower School eleven. Miss Latimer never says much, but I can see she's pleased with you. I'm so glad, because this really settles the question. You mustn't think of tennis again, but stick to cricket."

Patty was glad to have scored such a success. She had not been specially good at hockey during the winter, and was only a moderate tennis player, so it was pleasant to find one game in which she had a chance of excelling, and of gaining credit for her team as well as for herself. For once she tasted the sweets of popularity, and had the satisfaction of hearing even Vera Clifford offer her congratulations.

"I suppose I couldn't expect Muriel to do so," she thought. "She knows about it, though she wasn't watching the match, because I heard Cissie Gardiner telling her. She's the only one in the class who hasn't mentioned it. Of course it doesn't matter in the least; still, it would have been so nice, when I'm her own cousin, if she had said just a single word to show that she cared."

CHAPTER XII

Playing with Fire

THE Fourth Class, including the members of both upper and lower divisions, was by far the largest at The Priory, and, in the opinion of Miss Lincoln, the most unruly and difficult to manage. During her many years of teaching, she had always found that girls between fourteen and sixteen gave more than the usual amount of trouble. They were too old to be treated as children, and had already begun to set up standards of their own; indeed, they thought they knew most things a little better than their elders. They were impatient of discipline, yet their ideas were still crude and unformed, and they had not the judgment nor self-restraint which might be counted upon in the higher forms. It was a phase of character which she knew would soon pass, but it required judicious treatment, and she felt that a mistress needed to be both kind and firm to exercise the right influence at such a crisis in the young lives under her charge. Miss Harper, who was popular with her class, could always tame the most rebellious spirits, and maintain perfect order; but with Miss Rowe it was a totally different affair. She was not generally liked, and, taking advantage of her youth and lack of experience, many of the girls were as naughty as they dared, and defied her authority on every occasion. Amongst the ring-leaders in what may be called "the opposition", I regret to say Enid Walker held a foremost place. She was a very high-spirited, headstrong girl, who resented any restraint; she either took a violent fancy to people, or disliked them equally heartily: anyone who could gain her affection could lead her most easily, otherwise she was apt to prove so wayward as to cause a teacher to despair. Unfortunately Miss Rowe had not discovered the right way to manage Enid; for some time matters had been rather strained, and by the summer term it was a case of undeclared war between pupil and teacher.

"It doesn't matter what I say or do, Miss Rowe's always down on me!" declared Enid.

"Well, you really go rather too far sometimes," said Avis. "Miss Rowe knew perfectly well this morning that you dropped your atlas on purpose, and that it was you who tied Cissie's hair ribbon to her desk."

"Miss Rowe can be quite nice sometimes," said Patty. "When we were on the common yesterday, she found two new orchises, and gave them to me to press."

"Oh, you always manage to say something for everybody!" said Enid. "You're too good-natured, Patty. I can't bear Miss Rowe."

"But why?"

> "'I do not love thee, Doctor Fell,
> The reason why I cannot tell;
> But this I know, and know full well,
> I do not love thee, Doctor Fell,'"

quoted Enid. "That's how I feel, exactly."

"Perhaps she feels the same about you," suggested Winnie.

"Perhaps she does, but I don't care in the least. I don't like her voice, nor the cold way she looks at me and says, 'Now, Enid!' She's only an assistant teacher, and I'm not going to obey her as if she were Miss Lincoln or Miss Harper. She needn't expect it."

Certainly poor Miss Rowe found Enid a very trying pupil. Her attention was ever wandering, and she was invariably engaged in some mischief calculated to distract the rest of the class. She would sometimes give a wrong answer on purpose to raise a laugh; she could never lift the lid of her desk without letting it fall with a bang; and the contents of her pencil-box seemed always ready to disperse themselves over the floor. One morning the girls were having a lesson in grammar, and were diligently repeating Latin derivations and Anglo-Saxon suffixes, when some chance called Patty's attention to Enid. She noticed the latter open her desk stealthily, and draw out a tiny paper box, which she placed on her knee, and covered with her pocket handkerchief. Patty wondered what she was doing. It was evidently something which required great secrecy, for Enid glanced carefully round to see whether anyone was watching her; then, as nobody except Patty appeared to be looking, she drew away a fold of her handkerchief, cautiously opened the little box, and out hopped a huge grasshopper, which bounded straight on to Cissie Gardiner's blouse. Patty was so fascinated by gazing at it, and wondering where its next leap would take it, that she started when Miss Rowe asked her a question, and for once failed with her answer.

"Ad, ante," she began, but could get no further. Her eyes were glued to Cissie's blouse, and Cissie, noticing she was the cause of Patty's hesitation, looked down at her sleeve, and sprang up with a scream.

"Take it off! Somebody take it off!" she entreated. At this point the grasshopper promptly hopped away, no one could see where. Each girl naturally thought it might be on herself, and, jumping up, shook her skirts frantically. The class was instantly in the greatest disorder. Ella Johnson and May Firth stood on their seats, loudly protesting their horror of all creeping or crawling insects.

"Don't let it come on me! Oh, don't!" wailed Kitty Harrison.

"It's there!" exclaimed Maud Greening.

"Where?"

"It's hopped on to Doris."

"Oh! It will go down my neck!" shrieked Doris.

"No, it's hopped off again."

"It's on Maggie Woodhall's desk."

"Catch it, Maggie!"

"I daren't! I daren't!"

"Squash it with your ruler."

"I couldn't! I hate squashing things!"

"It's gone again."

"It will be on me next!"

"There it is on Maggie's desk again."

"Girls! Girls! Calm yourselves and keep still!" cried Miss Rowe's measured voice. "Maggie, sit down at once!"

The teacher strode across the room, and, catching the grasshopper in her hand, put it safely out of the window, then turned again to her agitated class.

"Order!" she said sternly; and after waiting a few moments until her pupils had regained their self-control, she continued: "Who let loose that grasshopper?"

"I did, Miss Rowe," replied Enid, promptly.

"Then you will leave the room at once, Enid. You will take a bad mark for conduct, and you will learn two pages of Greek chronology, and repeat them to me to-morrow morning before nine o'clock. Go immediately!"

Enid obeyed with as much noise as she could; she was in a naughty frame of mind, and enjoyed banging the door after her. She did not greatly care about either the bad mark for conduct or the Greek chronology, though she had an uncomfortable qualm when it occurred to her that the episode might possibly come to Miss Lincoln's ears. For this once, however, she was safe. Miss Rowe was anxious to manage her troublesome class without constant reference to the headmistress, and thought it better not to report the affair. She determined, nevertheless, that Enid, being the centre of so much mischief, should move from her desk, and, instead of sitting in the second row from the back, should be in front, directly under her teacher's eye. She mentioned her wish to Miss Harper, who ordered Enid to change places with Beatrice Wynne, and to transfer her books to her new desk before the next morning. Enid was furious.

"I won't go!" she declared to her companions. "Not unless Miss Rowe drags me there."

"You'll have to!" said Avis.

"I don't know about that. No one can force me to do a thing I don't want, not even Miss Lincoln."

"Miss Lincoln would expel you if you didn't do what you were told."

"I shouldn't care!"

"Oh, Enid, don't be silly! It can't make such a difference where you sit. I'll help you to move all your books, and put your new desk tidy," said Patty, hoping to pour oil on the troubled waters, and adding: "You'll have one advantage. You'll be close to Miss Harper in the botany class, and she'll hand you the specimens first. I wish I might change instead of you. I always envied Beatrice when she was pulling off petals, and we were craning our necks to try and look."

"It's easy enough to see the bright side for somebody else," grumbled Enid.

"Let us have our removal now," continued Patty, wisely taking no notice. "Beatrice is quite ready; aren't you, Beatrice? We'll lay all the things on the seat, and dust the desk inside before we put them in."

"I wouldn't do it for anybody but you," said Enid, allowing herself to be persuaded.

Beatrice soon emptied her desk, and it did not take very long to arrange the books in their new quarters. The alteration was effected almost before Enid realized it, and the storm which Patty had dreaded for her friend's sake was avoided. Nevertheless, Patty was not easy about Enid.

"She'll be getting into serious trouble some day," she thought. "I wish she would behave better in Miss Rowe's classes. Things can't always go on like this, and if Miss Rowe were to tell her to report herself in the library, I don't believe even Enid would like to face Miss Lincoln and find her really angry. I know I shouldn't."

It seemed no use for Patty to try remonstrances. Enid only laughed, and would not listen to her.

"Patty, you're a dear!" she declared. "I love you the best of any girl I know, but even you can't persuade me to like Miss Rowe. It's no use. We're flint and steel, or frost and fire; or oil and water, or anything else you can name that oughtn't to go together, and won't mix. The very tone of her voice annoys me."

"Why should it?"

"It's so prim. The way she pokes out her chin and says 'Enid!' is most disagreeable. It always makes me want to be naughty. Yes, it does; don't shake your head. I've told you a hundred times I'm not good like you, and I simply can't be. I'm like a bottle of soda-water with the cork popped, and I have to fizz over sometimes."

It was unfortunate that Enid should have taken such a dislike to her teacher, for she kept up a state of ill-feeling among the girls which otherwise would probably have died away. Absurd trifles were magnified and made much of, and ridiculous grievances were nursed and cherished. One day Miss Rowe set the upper division a grammar exercise consisting of two questions. The first was long and very difficult; it was on the origin of the English language, and required a certain knowledge of various Anglo-Saxon roots, a list of words derived from ancient British, and some account of the Norman-French period. The second and shorter question was simply a sentence to be parsed. No one in the class had a good memory for derivations. Fourteen out of the fifteen members spent the half-hour racking their brains and biting the ends of their pens in vain endeavours to complete their answers to Question 1, so that when it was time to hand in their exercise books, they had written very little, and that little was mostly wrong. The exercises were corrected and returned the next day, and each girl, with the solitary exception of Ella Johnson, found she had received a bad mark.

"It's too disgusting!" said Beatrice Wynne. "I don't believe even Miss Rowe herself could have answered that question without looking at the book."

"How did you manage it, Ella? You're the only one who's scraped through," asked Avis.

"I didn't attempt it," said Ella. "I did the parsing instead."

"You mean to say you didn't do Question 1 at all?" exclaimed Kitty Harrison.

"No, not I."

"How abominably unfair!" cried Enid. "I thought everybody had to begin with the first question. All the rest of us took so long over it, that we hadn't time for the parsing, and yet we got bad marks, and you, who hadn't even tried, got a good mark. It's just like Miss Rowe's meanness."

"It's really too bad," said Winnie. "Someone ought to go to Miss Rowe and ask her about it."

"Yes, so they ought."

"Who will, then?"

Nobody volunteered for the disagreeable task, and Avis suggested that Winnie herself might be suitable.

"I daren't, after the snubbing I got yesterday," said Winnie. "She wouldn't listen to me."

"I think it would be best if we were to draw lots," said Enid.

"No, don't draw lots, it seems like gambling," said Avis. "Suppose we count as we do for games? Stand in a circle, and I'll begin. Are you ready?"

"The first one who gets 'out' will have to go and tell Miss Rowe what we think, then," agreed Enid.

"'One, two, three, four, Jenny at the cottage door," began Avis. "'Eating cherries off a plate, five, six, seven, eight. One, two, three, out goes *she*.' Why, it's you, Winnie, after all."

"I wish it wasn't," groaned Winnie. "However, I suppose I shall have to go. Miss Rowe's in the studio, so I'll ask her now and get it over."

"Tell her we don't think it's fair," said Enid.

"And that Ella ought to have a bad mark too," said Kitty Harrison.

"Oh, you mean thing! It's not my fault," protested the indignant Ella.

"You can say we might all have done the parsing if we'd begun it first," said Beatrice.

"And don't forget to say there wouldn't have been time to answer two such long questions," said Maggie Woodhall.

"I'll do the best I can, but don't expect too much," replied Winnie. "Stay here, all of you, till I come back."

Winnie returned in about five minutes with a doleful face. "It's no use," she assured the girls, "I can't make Miss Rowe understand the point at all. She would only say: 'You wrote a very ill-prepared exercise, which did not deserve a good mark, and if you think I am going to excuse bad work you are quite mistaken'."

"It's just what I expected," declared Enid. "Miss Rowe carries everything with such a high hand, she won't take the trouble to listen properly when one tries to explain."

"It's a shame!" said all the girls, indignantly.

"I wish we could find some way of paying her out," said Enid.

"What could we do?"

"Let me think. I know! Suppose we none of us say 'Good morning' to her when she comes into the schoolroom to-morrow to take the register."

"Oh, yes! That would be splendid, and then she would see our opinion of her."

"Every girl must vow she won't say it, even you, Patty!"

"I think you're very silly," said Patty, "but I shan't be there myself. I always have my music lesson at nine o'clock on Friday mornings."

"So much the better," said Enid. "You were the only one I thought might spoil it. Will everybody else promise?"

All gave the required assent. The girls were anxious to air their grievance, and this seemed the most feasible way of showing their teacher their displeasure. At five minutes to nine on the following morning, they were seated in their places waiting for the second bell to ring. Miss Rowe entered punctually, and turning to the class as usual said: "Good morning".

There was no reply. She waited a moment in much astonishment.

"Good morning, girls," she said again.

Still there was dead silence in the room.

"I will give you one more chance. I cannot believe that you can be so deliberately and intentionally discourteous. Good morning, girls."

What would have happened at this juncture, whether the girls would have still persisted in defying their teacher, and so have obliged her to report their conduct to Miss Lincoln, or whether they would have given way with an ill grace, it is impossible to say. Fortunately for all concerned, Miss Harper was rather earlier than usual that day, and arriving in the schoolroom exactly at the critical moment, she saved the situation. Her greeting was answered by a chorus of "Good morning", which might be intended for both mistresses. Miss Rowe had the good sense to take no further notice, and to proceed at once to mark the register; and as she did not refer to the subject afterwards, the girls felt doubtful whether their little mutiny had been quite so effective as they had meant it to be.

"I wish Miss Rowe wasn't so horribly particular," said Avis, tidying her possessions ruefully a few days afterwards. "She says she's going to look at all our desks this afternoon, and give forfeits for any that are in a muddle. I haven't rummaged to the back of mine for ever so long. I scarcely know what's in it. Why, what's this? It's actually a box of fusees. I remember now, I brought them from home. I'd quite forgotten I had them."

"Oh, do give them to me!" cried Enid. "They make such a lovely hissing noise, I like to hear them go off."

"You'd better not strike them in class, then," replied Avis.

"Do you dare me to?"

"Why, even you wouldn't do such a risky thing!"

"Oh! What would Miss Rowe say if you did it in the very middle of Euclid?" said Cissie Gardiner, with round eyes of delighted horror.

"Then I will, just to show you I dare. I'm not afraid of Miss Rowe!" declared Enid, appropriating the box and putting it in her pocket.

The girls laughed, not believing for a moment that she really intended to carry out her threat. The bell rang, Miss Rowe entered, and lessons began before they had time to say anything more about it. Euclid was not a favourite subject with the Upper Fourth. It was considered dry, and the half-hour devoted to it was regarded as more or less of a penance. In the very middle of the fifth proposition, when Miss Rowe had changed the letters on the blackboard, and was endeavouring to make Vera Clifford grasp the principle of the reasoning, instead of merely repeating the problem by rote, Enid's head was bent low over her desk, and her fingers appeared to be busy with something.

"Y G K = D F O," droned Vera in a melancholy voice.

Suddenly there was a striking sound, and a loud, long hiss.

"Oh! oh! oh!" came in a subdued chorus from all sides.

"Enid, what are you doing?" cried Miss Rowe, sharply.

For answer naughty Enid held up the hissing fusee in a kind of daring triumph, but as she raised her head her long curly hair, which was floating loose, brushed against the burning spark, and in an instant blazed up, setting fire also to the sleeve of her thin lawn blouse. With a wild shriek she dropped the fusee, and, springing from her seat, would have tried in her terror to rush from the room had she not been prevented by Miss Rowe, who, with admirable presence of mind, seized the duster from the blackboard, and with only that and her bare hands succeeded in stifling the flames. The whole class was in a panic. Jean Bannerman ran at once for Miss Hall, the teacher in the next room, and in a very short space of time Miss Lincoln herself arrived on the scene. Finding that Enid and Miss Rowe were the only two hurt, she carried them off at once to apply first aid until a doctor could be summoned, leaving Miss Hall to try and calm the agitated girls. Cissie Gardiner was sobbing hysterically, and all were offering versions of the accident in such a state of excitement, that it was difficult to understand their accounts.

"Enid Walker lighted a fusee?" repeated Miss Hall, almost incredulously. "Then she alone is responsible for this unhappy occurrence. I can only trust that neither she nor Miss Rowe is seriously injured. Girls, go back to your desks. I must return now to my own class, but I will send a prefect to you as soon as possible. I trust to your good feeling to work in silence at your preparation for to-morrow."

Miss Rowe and Enid were taken to the sanatorium, which was always kept in readiness to receive urgent cases. Both were suffering greatly from the shock: Miss Rowe's hands were badly scorched, and Enid had a severe burn on her arm and also on her neck. The doctor, having completed his dressings, ordered them both to be kept very quiet, and not to receive visitors until he gave his permission. It was several days, therefore, before Enid was allowed to see any of her school-fellows, and when the nurse at last declared that she might have a friend to spend half an hour with her, she fixed her choice at once upon Patty. The latter had been two or three times a day to the sanatorium to enquire how the invalids were progressing, so it was with great eagerness that she now knocked at the door. She was admitted by the nurse, and after a warning not to excite her companion, was shown to Enid's room. Enid was lying on the sofa, her arm swathed in bandages; some of her pretty hair had been cut away, and her face looked white, with dark circles round her eyes, as if she had not slept. Patty, after a rapturous greeting, sat down on a chair by her side, and began to tell her the school news.

"Everybody sent all kinds of messages," she said. "It seems so funny in class without either you or Miss Rowe. Have you seen Miss Rowe? Are her hands very bad?"

"They're both bandaged up," replied Enid. "She won't be able to use them for some time. Wasn't it brave of her to rush at me with the duster? Do you know, she's been so nice. We had a long talk last night, and she told me ever so many things. She meant to go to Girton when she left school, but her father lost all his money, and she had to begin to teach at once, so that she could help a younger brother. She's paying for his education herself, and he's doing splendidly at his school, and she's so proud of him, and hopes he may win a scholarship. If I'd only known all this, I wouldn't have made it so hard for her. I'm as sorry for that now as I am about her hands being burnt."

"I always thought Miss Rowe was nicer than you imagined. I'm so glad you've found it out," said Patty.

"I expect she's one of those people who improve on acquaintance," continued Enid. "I couldn't bear her at one time, and now I believe I'm going to like her immensely. You can't think how jolly she can make herself. I'll never be naughty in her class again, or let anybody else be, if I can help it. On my honour I won't!"

Enid was as good as her word. When she and Miss Rowe were well enough to again take their places in school, the young teacher found, to her surprise, that all her trouble with the Upper Fourth was at an end. The girls regarded her in the light of a heroine, and her new popularity gave her an influence over them which her efforts at strict discipline had not been able to gain.

"She seems quite different," said Winnie, voicing the feelings of the class. "She's far pleasanter than she used to be, and now she doesn't order us about so much, we don't seem to want to do so many things we oughtn't. She's really very pretty, you know; her nose is just perfect, and her hair is so thick and fair. Of course she can't compare with Miss Harper, but still I like her ever so much better than I did before, and I vote we give her a tremendous clapping on Speech Day."

CHAPTER XIII

The School Picnic

Towards the middle of July the girls at The Priory began to look forward with eager anticipation to the annual picnic. In the minds of most it was the great event of the summer term, and eclipsed even Speech Day. Patty, who had not yet experienced the joys of such an excursion, was anxious to learn something about it, and made many enquiries of her friends.

"It's the loveliest fun," said Avis. "We have special saloon carriages engaged on the train, and lovely baskets of lunch, and Miss Lincoln lets us buy toffee and chocolates if there are any shops. I wonder where we shall go this year, and if it will be to the country or the seaside. Has anyone heard?"

"Phyllis Chambers said she believed it was to be Moorcliffe," said Winnie.

"Where's that?"

"It's a dear little seaside place near Chelstone. There's a nice sandy shore, and Phyllis says she shouldn't be surprised if we were allowed to take our costumes with us and bathe."

"Oh, how glorious! I do hope we shall."

"I believe it depends on the tide," said Winnie.

"Why on the tide? How absurd!"

"No, it's not absurd. The sea goes out very far at Moorcliffe, and leaves a large sandy bay. You don't want to walk half a mile to the water. If the tide's up in the morning, and we can get our dip then, it will be quite right, because there will be time for our costumes to dry afterwards in the sun; but if it's not high water till afternoon, we shall have to do without our swim. It would be impossible to carry back more than seventy dripping bathing-dresses."

"Unless we chartered a tank for them and put them in the luggage van," laughed Enid. "I hope the tide will be nice and accommodating. Hasn't anybody got an almanac?"

"Miss Lincoln is planning it all out, and is to tell us on Saturday."

"I don't think it depends entirely on the tide," said Beatrice Wynne. "I was talking to Miss Latimer, and she says she knows of a splendid pool under the cliff, which is always quite deep enough to swim in at low water. She's going to tell Miss Lincoln about it."

"If we don't arrange for Moorcliffe, we shall probably go to Bradley, and look over the Castle," said Maggie Woodhall.

"I hope not," said Cissie Gardiner. "I've seen several castles, and they're all alike. You walk on the battlements, and peep down the well, which is half filled with rubbish and ferns, and an old woman unlocks the dungeon, and shows you a rusty chain, and then you eat sandwiches in the courtyard. I'd far rather go to the sea."

Cissie's wish was gratified, for on Saturday morning Miss Lincoln gave the welcome announcement that she had decided the picnic should be at Moorcliffe on the following Thursday, provided that the weather was favourable, and that no unforeseen event occurred in the meantime.

"Miss Lincoln always puts in a warning note of that kind," said Enid. "I wonder what she expects to happen. Does she imagine we shall all catch scarlet fever, or break our legs, before Thursday?"

"I should hope not, but of course it might be wet. If it's a pouring day, we're to go on Friday instead," said Avis.

"To-day, Sunday, Monday, Tuesday, and Wednesday to get through," said Jean. "It's a frightfully long time. I feel as if Thursday would never come."

"So do I. I should like to go to bed, and sleep straight through till Thursday."

"You lazy girl! Suppose you didn't wake, and we left you behind?"

"You wouldn't do that," declared Avis. "I shall be up first of all, you'll see."

In spite of the girls' impatience, the longed-for Thursday came at last, and proved such a fine, clear, beautiful day, that there was not the slightest hesitation as to whether they should start or not. Avis fulfilled her promise of early rising by getting up to watch the dawn, and tried to make her sleepy room mates share her enthusiasm, an attention which they scarcely appreciated when they discovered that she had roused them three hours too soon. Long before the usual bell rang everybody was up and dressed, which did not bring breakfast any the quicker, though it allowed the girls time to work off some of their spirits by a run round the garden. Punctually at a quarter to nine o'clock a row of omnibuses arrived to convey the seventy-three pupils and their ten teachers to the station. Each girl carried her bathing costume and towel in a neat parcel, and large hampers of lunch were in readiness.

"Miss Lincoln's taking the cricket tent," announced Cissie Gardiner. "There it is, all wrapped up with its poles and pegs. Miss Latimer and Miss Rowe are going to put it up on the beach, and then we can undress and dress there again when we bathe. It's not very big. I'm sure it can't possibly hold more than six of us at a time, so we shall have to go in relays, and be very quick."

Patty felt at the high-water mark of bliss when she found herself seated on the top of an omnibus between Enid and Jean, with Avis and Winnie close by. She could have wished the drive longer, but when they reached the station, and found the saloon carriages ready for them, labelled "Special Excursion—Reserved", she was as anxious to get into the train as she had been to remain on the omnibus. There were, of course, many little excitements. Winnie nearly left the parcel containing her bathing-dress on the seat near the booking office, only remembering it just in time; Maggie Woodhall's hat blew away over the line, and had to be recovered by the guard; and one of the luncheon baskets fell off the truck as the porter was wheeling it along the platform, much to Miss Lincoln's dismay, till she discovered it was luckily not the one which held the breakables. Each mistress was to be personally responsible for her own class, and for the day the six prefects were given as full powers of authority as the teachers; so Miss Lincoln hoped that with so many people to look after them, her lively pupils might find no opportunity of getting into mischief, or running into danger. All were able to take their places at once in the carriages which had been waiting for them in a siding at the station, and were shunted on to the Chelstone train when it arrived. The porters banged the doors with their usual vigour, the guard waved his green flag, and at last they were off for their delightful excursion. It was less than an hour's journey to Moorcliffe, so by half-past ten the entire school was walking in a procession through the small village, across the cliff, and down on to the beach. The tide unfortunately was low, so Miss Lincoln was glad to avail herself of Miss Latimer's knowledge of the place to find the cove where there was a convenient bathing pool. It was some little distance along the shore, and the girls were much tempted to linger to pick up shells or sea urchins; but the prefects urged them sternly on, assuring them that they would find plenty more of such treasures, and that time was passing quickly by.

"When you consider how small the tent is, and how many of us have to take it in turns to use it, you'll understand we need the whole morning for our bathe," said Phyllis Chambers.

They at last reached the sheltered nook among the rocks which Miss Latimer had chosen. The sea, retreating far into the distance, had here left a wide and fairly deep pool, through which flowed one of the many channels that intersected the bay. It was a pleasant spot, far enough from the village to promise retirement, and the sparkling water lapping gently in the sunshine looked inviting. Aided by a band of willing workers, Miss Latimer and Miss Rowe soon erected the tent; the girls effected their changes of costume with lightning speed, and in half an hour a passing stranger might have imagined the coast to be invaded by an army of mermaids. Jean, who had brought her camera, took several snapshots of the lively scene.

"It reminds me of pictures I've seen of colonies of seals basking about on the rocks," she declared. "Now, Patty, put yourself in a picturesque attitude. I wish I dare ask Miss Rowe to let down her lovely hair, I'm sure it would look so nice."

"Violet Chambers is swimming on her back," said Enid. "I'm so glad to have the opportunity of watching her. I heard she could do it, but we never get a chance to see the Second Class girls in the bath."

"And Mabel Morgan is trying to make a wheel," said Winnie. "Oh, look at her! Isn't she clever? There! She's come to grief over it. I expected she would."

"I haven't any accomplishments," said Avis. "I can only paddle round and round the pool and float. I wish I were in the channel over there, and could swim for a couple of miles."

"I heard Miss Lincoln tell Miss Latimer she was very glad the tide was low, because it was absolutely safe here, and if we were in the real sea, she should not know a moment's freedom from anxiety until she saw us all out again."

"Miss Lincoln is quite ridiculous! What harm could happen to us? Of course the pool is better fun than the swimming bath at The Priory, but it's nothing to feeling yourself on big waves."

"We're going to Devonshire for our summer holiday, and I shall be able to have some glorious swimming there, I expect," said May Firth.

"You'll have to mind not to get into a current," said Ella Johnson. "We were staying in Cornwall last year, and my brother was nearly carried out to sea by one. He declared it must have been the Gulf Stream; it was so tremendously strong, it whirled him along, and he felt quite helpless. All he could do was to float and to call, hoping somebody might hear him. No one did for a long time, and he had drifted ever so far from land, when at last a boat was passing, and some fishermen picked him up. They told him it was very dangerous to swim there, when he didn't know the coast."

"It's all right if you don't get cramp," said Avis. "That must be dreadful. Once when we spent our holidays at Whitby we had such an adventure. We were walking along the shore, and we saw a young lady swimming a little distance out. Suddenly she flung up her arms and shrieked, and went down into the water. My father threw off his coat and his boots, and swam to the spot where she came up. He managed to catch hold of her by her hair, and get her back to land. She was quite insensible, and I thought she must be dead; but my uncle, who's a doctor, was with us, and he immediately began the treatment for the drowned, just like Miss Latimer teaches us in the swimming lessons. I helped to work her arms up and down and to rub her, and at last she opened her eyes. We were so relieved. She called at our lodgings afterwards to thank us, and said she had gone for a little afternoon dip alone; and she supposed the water must have been colder than usual, because all at once she felt a terrible pain in her leg, and could not move. She said it was the most awful sensation to feel she was sinking, and not to be able to save herself."

"It was lucky for her that your father was close by to rescue her!"

"Yes, and Uncle Arthur too, to bring her round afterwards. I don't think it's very safe for girls to go swimming alone."

No mermaids could have had a pleasanter time idling about in the pool than Patty and her friends. They tried various performances in fancy swimming, which, however, were quite unsuccessful, though they all assisted to hold each other up during the experiments. They were in the midst of a frantic effort to dance the Lancers in two feet of water, when Miss Latimer called to them to come at once; and as the limited accommodation of the bathing tent necessitated that the girls must make their toilets in relays, they were obliged reluctantly to tear themselves away, and in due course join the others, who were sitting on the sand letting their loose hair dry in the sun and wind. Everybody was very ready to open the luncheon baskets at half-past twelve. The sea air had given fine appetites, and the provisions vanished steadily. Each class had brought its own special hamper, and there was a great deal of laughter when those of the Third and Fifth Classes got changed by mistake, the thirteen indignant members of the former only receiving the amount which had been intended for ten. The upper and lower divisions of the Fourth feasted separately, the one under the auspices of Miss Harper, and the other with Miss Rowe, as it would have been impossible to pack lunch for twenty-two girls in one hamper, unless, as Enid suggested, they had used a clothes basket for the purpose. After lunch, Miss Lincoln insisted that everybody should take half an hour's quiet rest lying on the beach.

"Many of you were awake at daylight," she said, "and you have been racing about and exciting yourselves since before breakfast-time. I am afraid you will all be thoroughly tired out by evening, so I forbid anyone to speak; and if you can go to sleep, so much the better."

I hardly think Miss Lincoln expected her injunctions to be absolutely obeyed; at any rate, a certain amount of whispering went on among the girls, who collected in little groups to take the required repose, while a low laugh every now and then did not indicate sound slumber. Avis piled up a pillow of sand, and closed her eyes complacently, until she found Winnie was tickling the end of her nose with a piece of seaweed; Enid lay curled up under the shadow of a rock, looking at her watch every few minutes; and Jean and Patty played a silent game of noughts and crosses on slabs of smooth stone. The moment the half-hour was finished the girls sprang up, and commenced to chatter with renewed avidity, showing in their own lively fashion that they were not yet tired, however they might feel by the end of the day. The classes separated during the afternoon, some going for walks on the headland, and others strolling farther along the beach, searching for cockles on the sandbank, or throwing stones at a mark. They all met at four o'clock for tea at the small hotel on the edge of the cliff, where tables and forms had been set out in the garden, and the innkeeper and his wife and two daughters were busily bustling about, carrying plates of cakes and buns, jugs of milk, and trays full of cups and saucers, to meet the requirements of their army of young guests. It was a merry meal, for everybody was full of jokes and fun. Miss Harper told amusing stories, and Miss Lincoln asked riddles, and Miss Rowe forgot she was keeping order, and chatted almost like one of the girls themselves.

"I could sit here all afternoon," said Enid, "just watching the sea and the boats and the people down on the shore below. If I could only get up a second appetite, I should like to begin tea over again."

"You can have some more if you like. Miss Lincoln doesn't limit you," laughed Avis.

"No, thank you. The copybooks say: 'Never attempt impossibilities'. I shall go and sit on the edge of the cliff."

"Come with me," said Winnie, "and we'll have a game of golf just to ourselves, with two sticks and an indiarubber ball. You can't think what fun it is. I was trying on the common a little while ago. Will you come too, Patty?"

"No, thanks," said Patty. "I should only spoil sport. I mean to go down on to the sands again. You can call to me when you've finished, and perhaps I'll come up; but I won't promise, because I like the shore the very best of all."

CHAPTER XIV

On the Rocks

"Our train will start at half-past six," said Miss Lincoln, when tea was finished, and the girls were standing in little groups in the hotel garden, wondering what to do next. "All who like may go on to the beach again, or on to the cliffs, but no one must walk farther than the white farm near the flagstaff. You must return immediately you are told, and be at the station by a quarter past six."

The girls dispersed, some to wander along the shore to find a few more shells, mermaids' purses, or strips of ribbon seaweed; some to climb to the top of the cliff by the flagstaff; and others to play games on a piece of common near the white farm that Miss Lincoln had appointed as a boundary beyond which they must not venture. Patty, who was hunting for sea anemones in the small pools among the rocks, noticed Muriel and her friends, Maud, Vera, and Kitty, hurrying as fast as they could along the beach in the opposite direction from the village.

"Where are you going?" called Phyllis Chambers, who was engaged in taking down the bathing tent.

"Oh! nowhere in particular," they replied, stopping as if they had been rather caught; "only just for a little stroll, to say good-bye to the waves."

"You mustn't go beyond the next point of rock; Miss Lincoln said so."

"Miss Lincoln said nothing about the shore. She said the white farm on the cliff," replied Maud, rather sulkily.

"Well, that rock is exactly underneath the farm."

"We were only going to peep round the point. It wouldn't take five minutes," said Muriel.

"I can't allow it, all the same," said Phyllis, firmly.

"I'm sure Miss Lincoln never meant——" began Kitty Harrison, but she was interrupted by Phyllis.

"Miss Lincoln has put me in authority for this afternoon. I have her orders, and I tell you you're not to go."

Looking very cross and disconsolate, the four girls sat down on the sand a little distance away, to grumble and discuss the situation.

"I don't believe Miss Lincoln meant exactly what she said," declared Kitty.

"I'm sure she didn't. It's only Phyllis who's so proud of being prefect, and likes to show her authority," agreed Maud.

"I don't see why we should do as she tells us; she's only a schoolgirl like ourselves," said Vera.

"I expect she wanted to be nasty, and pay us out for what happened last week in the gymnasium," said Muriel.

"It's too bad!"

"It's an absolute shame!"

"Suppose we were to go after all," suggested Vera tentatively.

"But Phyllis would stop us."

"She won't see. She's taking the tent poles and walking up that path towards the hotel. She'll be round the corner in half a minute."

"Why, so she is!"

"If we're quick we could be beyond the point before she comes back."

"Then come along at once."

"Yes, don't let us waste a moment."

The four girls jumped up, and, hurrying off, went away round the rock with such record speed, that by the time Phyllis returned to fetch the remainder of the tent they were well out of sight. Imagining that they must have walked down the beach towards the village, Phyllis did not trouble to go and look for them, so the only person who knew the real direction they had taken was Patty, who happened to have overheard most of the conversation, and to have seen their hasty flight. Having examined as many sea anemones as she cared to, Patty climbed up a steep little track on to the cliff again, and spent a blissful half-hour by herself, lying in the sunshine on a bed of purple heath, watching the white sails of the boats in the distance, and a steamer far out on the horizon. From her point of lookout she had a very good view over the whole of the large bay. How fast the tide was flowing in! The sandbanks, which only ten minutes ago had gleamed yellow in the sunshine, were now covered with water, and a huge white wave appeared at the mouth of the estuary, advancing with threatening speed.

"It must be the tidal wave that Phyllis spoke about," thought Patty. "She told us how dangerous it is on this coast, how it comes in with a great rush, as fast as a man can run, and floods all the bay quite suddenly. I expect that was the reason Miss Lincoln wouldn't let us go far along the beach this afternoon. Why! Surely that cannot be Muriel and the others such a long way out upon the sands! I thought they would have been back before now. Yes, it is! And their backs are turned to the sea! They're sauntering along as calmly as if the tide were going down instead of rising. Oh, why don't they look round and hurry?"

Patty sprang to her feet and waved her handkerchief frantically, but the girls were not looking in her direction, and took no notice. What was she to do? She felt, at all costs, they must be warned. She would be obliged to disregard Miss Lincoln's orders, and to go along the beach and tell them of their danger. There was not time to run back and ask permission. Nobody else was in sight, so she must decide on her own authority that it was expedient for once to disobey. Scrambling quickly on to the shore by an even more precipitous path than the one by which she had ascended, Patty made what haste she could along the sands towards her companions. She shouted to them while she was still a considerable distance off, but though they waved their hands in reply, they did not come any the faster.

"How stupid they are!" thought Patty. "Can't they see the water behind them? They walk as if they were strolling round the quad."

With an extra effort she hurried on, and reached them out of breath and panting.

"Why don't you make haste?" she gasped. "Didn't you hear me call?"

"It's all very well to say 'Make haste!'" replied Maud. "We can't get Muriel along."

"I've hurt my foot," said Muriel. "I slipped on a stone, and I think I must have sprained my ankle. It hurts dreadfully when I lean any weight upon it. Let me have your arm, Patty."

"Don't you see how fast the tide's rising?" said Patty, giving the asked-for assistance. "If we're not very quick we shall be surrounded."

"Why, so we shall!" exclaimed Vera. "I didn't notice it before. Come along at once. We must run."

"I can't run," said Muriel fretfully, "you know I can't. I can scarcely even limp as it is."

"You must," said Maud, taking her other arm; "that is, if you don't want to be drowned."

"Don't pull me, Maud," cried Muriel, "you're hurting me. Oh, I can't go any faster! My foot will give way underneath me."

"What are we to do?" said Kitty blankly. "The water's rushing round on both sides of us! If we don't get across that piece of sand in front directly, we shall be on an island."

"Let us make a chair of our hands," suggested Patty, "and try to carry Muriel. See, Maud! Clasp my wrists like this, and I'll clasp yours. Muriel, sit down! Now, then; one, two, let's step together."

"She's too heavy; I can't manage it!" exclaimed Maud, dropping her burden on to the sands.

"Then you try, Kitty."

"No, no! I'm not so strong as Maud. Oh, look at the water!"

"Come along, girls," shouted Vera, "we must run for our lives! It's no use our all being drowned."

"Maud! Kitty! Vera! You don't mean to leave me?" shrieked Muriel.

"Quick! Quick!" was the sole reply she received, as her three friends took to their heels, and, without even turning to look at her, dashed across the narrow belt of dry land which led between two channels to the safer bank of shingle beyond.

"The cowards! The mean cowards!" cried Muriel, white with anger and alarm. "Patty, are you going too?"

"Not without you," replied Patty, sturdily. "Here, I'll help you up, Muriel, and we must push on, even if we have to wade. Catch hold of my arm again, and try to walk."

"It hurts so; my foot won't hold me. Oh, the pain is so bad, I must stop for a minute!"

Patty looked round desperately. Their situation was indeed most dangerous. The one path to safety was already covered, and even if they were able to hurry on fast, it was doubtful whether they would be able to wade to the shore. They were cut off on every side, and their little island was each moment diminishing in size.

"We must climb on to these rocks," she exclaimed. "Let us scramble up the tallest; perhaps it may be above high-water mark. Put your arms round my neck, Muriel, and I'll carry you as well as I can."

Almost sinking under her cousin's weight, Patty staggered along till she reached the jagged, seaweed-covered rock, which she hoped might afford them a temporary place of security. Groaning with pain, Muriel managed with Patty's help to drag herself slowly to the summit.

"Why did I come?" she said. "It was all Vera's fault. She persuaded us to go, and then kept taking us a little farther and a little farther every time we wanted to turn back. We shall be drowned; I know we shall."

"I don't think so," returned Patty hopefully. "The top of the rock is quite dry, as if it weren't covered at high tide. I believe we shall be safe, only we may have to stop here for a very long while."

"Let us call for help," suggested Muriel.

Both girls shouted at the pitch of their voices again and again, but there was no response, except from the sea birds which they disturbed on the adjacent cliffs.

"THEY WERE CUT OFF ON EVERY SIDE"

"How long shall we have to stay here?" enquired Muriel presently.

"Why, until the water goes down again."

"When will it go down?"

"What time is it now?" asked Patty.

Muriel consulted the little watch which she wore in a strap on her wrist.

"Exactly six o'clock," she replied.

"Then it will be high tide about eight or nine, I suppose, and I don't think it will be low again until nearly midnight, or early in the morning."

"How dreadful! Won't anybody come to fetch us off?"

"I don't see how they could reach us. Look at the sea! It's rushing between the rocks like a mill-race. Any ordinary boat would be dashed to pieces, and there's no lifeboat at Moorcliffe."

Muriel shuddered. The water had indeed overflowed the whole of the sandbank, and now swirled in a foaming current round the foot of their retreat, rising every moment a little nearer to them. Following the tide had come a dense sea fog, that drifted down the bay, veiling the sun, and, creeping round the rock, wrapped the girls in its clammy, concealing folds, cutting them off effectually from all possibility of being seen from the neighbouring cliff. In a few minutes the whole prospect was blotted out; they seemed in a world of white mist, as absolutely isolated and alone as if they were in mid-ocean. Trembling with fear, Muriel turned to Patty.

"Do you think anybody knows where we are?" she asked.

"I can't say. Vera and the others would, of course, tell Miss Lincoln, but she wouldn't know exactly where to look, and no one could find us in this fog."

"Do you think the sea'll rise any higher?"

"Yes, a little. It can hardly be full tide yet."

"Patty! I don't know whether I shall be able to swim with my hurt foot. Suppose the water comes right over the rock, you won't leave me like the others did, will you?"

"Never!" said Patty, putting her arm round her cousin. "We'll either both get safely to land, or both go down together."

"Will you promise?"

"Faithfully."

"Thank you. I know you always keep your promises," said Muriel.

She did not speak again for a long time, but sat holding Patty's hand tightly, and gazing under a horrible fascination at the green, foam-flecked water that was creeping so stealthily nearer to them. How cold it looked, and how cruel! How easily it could swirl away their light weights, and dash them against those jagged points opposite, or sweep them out into the midst of those long waves, the white crests of which were just dimly visible through the wall of fog! Inch by inch it rose; it was only a foot now from the top of the rock, far above the line which they had supposed was high-water mark.

"I think we had better both take off our tennis shoes," said Patty. "If we're obliged to swim, you could perhaps manage to float, and I could pull you along."

"Patty, aren't you terribly afraid?"

"No, not very. Not so much as I thought I should be."

There was silence for a few minutes, and then Muriel said:

"I can't think how it is you're not afraid."

"Because God can take care of us here as well as anywhere else," answered Patty, quietly.

"Do you really think He will?"

"I'm going to ask Him now."

"Then so will I," said Muriel, kneeling by her side on the rock.

"Lighten our darkness, we beseech Thee, O Lord, and by Thy great mercy defend us from all perils and dangers of this night."

How often they had repeated the familiar collect in church or at evening prayers in the big schoolroom at The Priory, sometimes with little thought for its meaning; and how different it sounded now in the midst of the real peril and danger that surrounded them! A great wave came suddenly dashing up and poured over their feet, and the two trembling girls looked with white faces as the shoes, which they had taken off and laid beside them, were swept away and lost in the depths below. Many fresh thoughts came to Muriel then—thoughts such as had rarely troubled her before. In the mist and the rushing water her old standards seemed to be slipping from her; wealth and position felt of slight value compared to those better things about which she had hitherto cared so little: and I think, with the surging tide, some of her old self passed away, and left a new self born in its place.

"It's going down!" cried Patty at last. "That one wave was the high-water mark. Look! It's certainly lower than it was."

"Then we're saved!" exclaimed Muriel; and, breaking down utterly, she covered her face with her hands, and burst into a storm of tears.

The tide was undoubtedly on the turn; each wave seemed less forceful than the last, and though they were still surrounded by water, and likely to be kept prisoners for many hours yet, they could consider themselves free from danger, and feel that their lives had been spared. Time crept slowly on; fortunately, owing to the length of the July day, it was not yet dark, but the fog had not lifted, and they were not able to see even so far as the adjoining rocks. Their clothes were wet through with spray, and they felt damp, and chilly, and forlorn. Both girls had been tired out with their long day's pleasure before they were caught by the tide, and the hours of waiting seemed interminable. Muriel, exhausted with fright and exposure, clung piteously to Patty, crying quietly, and the latter gave her what comfort she had to offer.

"The water's halfway down the rock already," she said. "In another hour we may be able to reach the shore, if only the mist would clear."

"My foot still hurts," said Muriel. "I don't believe I shall be able to limp a step."

"Perhaps a boat will come to find us, now the tide's not so high. I'm sure Miss Lincoln would send somebody to look."

"You don't think she would go home without us, then?"

"Oh, no! I'm quite certain she wouldn't. Someone would miss us, and then she would ask who had seen us last."

"Do you think Kitty and Maud and Vera would tell? Perhaps they'd be ashamed of having left us."

"They'd be obliged to tell. I expect if it hadn't been for the fog we should have been found before. If you leant your head against me, could you go to sleep?"

"No, not with the water still so near," said Muriel, shuddering. "I must just sit still, and wait, and wait, and wait."

Half an hour more passed; the girls were too weary to care to talk, but at last Muriel spoke again.

"Patty," she said, suddenly, "I want to tell you a secret. It's something I ought to have told long ago, only I didn't dare. That Cæsar translation belonged to me."

"I thought it did," said Patty, calmly.

"You thought so! Oh, Patty! How did you know?"

"Because I saw you slip it into your desk that afternoon I came so unexpectedly into the schoolroom. I recognized the green cover the moment Miss Harper held it up."

"And yet you never said anything about it?"

"No."

"Not to anybody? Not even to Enid?"

"No, not even to Enid. I wasn't certain, and if I had been I wouldn't have told."

"I've been wretched about it!" said Muriel. "I never intended you to get blamed, but I daren't confess it was mine."

"Who gave you the book?" asked Patty.

"Horace. He used it himself once, and those were his initials in it, H. P. for Horace Pearson; and of course everyone believed it meant Patty Hirst, because the two letters were interlaced, and could be read either way."

"I'm sorry it was Horace's. I thought better of him," groaned Patty.

"I'm afraid we're neither of us as conscientious as you," said Muriel. "I used to prepare my Latin with it. I don't know how I could be so silly as to leave it lying about."

"Perhaps it's as well you did," said Patty, gravely, "or it might never have been found out."

"I'm dreadfully sorry now," said Muriel. "I wouldn't do it again. I'm so glad Miss Harper burnt it. It was most unfortunate it should be fixed upon you. I always told the girls you were innocent."

"I don't think many of them believed it was mine."

"A few did, or at any rate pretended they did. Well, I'll set it all straight when I get back to school. It'll be hateful to tell Miss Harper, but it's the one thing I can do to make up, and I will."

Another half-hour had passed, and a slight breeze blowing from the sea began at length to disperse the fog, which, thinning a little, revealed the outline of the cliffs on the landward side. The sun had long ago set, but still showed such a bright glow on the western horizon, that it was light enough to see that the sandbank was almost clear, and the water flowing from it in broad channels.

"I think we might leave our rock now," said Patty. "Perhaps if we wade we could reach the shore before it gets quite dark. Can you manage if I help you?"

Muriel climbed painfully down, and taking Patty's arm, began to limp her way over the sands.

"It's half-past ten," she said, "and our train was to leave at half-past six. All the others will have gone home ages ago. I don't know what we must do, even if we get to land."

"Somebody's sure to be waiting for us," said Patty. "Why, I believe I can see a boat over there in the distance. Look! To your left, where the mist is blowing away."

"It is!" exclaimed Muriel, in much excitement. "A fishing boat, with three men in it. Let us call as loudly as we can."

The two girls joined in a wild "Halloo!" and to their great relief were at once answered by a shout in reply. The boat turned her course and made for the sandbank, and in a few minutes a bronzed old seaman had leaped over the gunwale and waded through the channel to their rescue.

"Why, little misses, you've got yourselves in a fine fix!" he said, by way of greeting. "Here we've bin a-lookin' for you for a matter of four hours; just hangin' about in the fog, we was, and shoutin' every now and then on the off chance of your hearin' us. I ne'er thought we'd find you safe and sound, I didn't. Bin up the rock, you say? Ay, them rocks is never covered. If I'd only knowed you was there! We'd a' seen you long since, if it hadn't a' bin for the fog."

He lifted Muriel in his arms, and, carrying her as easily as if she had been a baby, waded with her to the boat, returning afterwards for Patty.

"You're nigh dead beat, both on you," he said, sympathetically. "It's give you a rare fright, I'll be bound, and us too! Your teacher's half crazed after you, poor thing! She'll be main glad to see you back, she will that!"

It was indeed with a feeling of intense relief and thankfulness that Miss Lincoln welcomed the missing pair as the boat drew up on the beach at Moorcliffe. The hours of their absence had been a time of such anxiety and suspense as she had not experienced before with any of her pupils. One look at her face showed them what she had suffered on their behalf.

"Thank God you are safe!" she cried, as she took them in her arms and kissed them.

All the school had returned to The Priory, only Miss Harper remaining with Miss Lincoln; and as the last train had left, the latter made arrangements to spend the night at the hotel. The girls were cold and wet, and much in need of food and rest; so they were only too thankful to be put to bed at once, instead of starting on a railway journey. The headmistress would allow very little talk that night about what had happened, reserving what she had to say for a future occasion; and Muriel, who knew there was a painful explanation in store for her, was not sorry that it should be deferred.

"I shall be in dreadful trouble to-morrow," she said to Patty as they lay in bed, "and I deserve it, I know. I'm going to make a clean breast of everything, the Cæsar translation and several other things, and then perhaps I shall feel better, and make a fresh start. I haven't said 'Thank you' to you, Patty, because I really don't know how; but you've been an absolute trump, and I shall tell Miss Lincoln so. I shan't ever forget it. Good-night!"

CHAPTER XV

Speech Day

A NIGHT's rest did much to restore the two girls after their terrible experience on the rocks. By next morning, though Muriel's foot still hurt her when she walked, they were both well enough to return to school, where, as you may imagine, they had many things to relate to their companions, who were brimming over with eagerness to hear a full and detailed account of the whole adventure. Muriel had a long interview with Miss Lincoln in the library, from which she emerged with red eyes, and, escaping from her friends, retired to her bedroom, and, drawing the curtains of her cubicle, spent the afternoon alone. She was strangely softened and subdued; she said little when Vera, Kitty, and Maud stammered out their apologies for deserting her on the shore, and appeared so preoccupied and thoughtful at tea-time, that she scarcely noticed when the others spoke to her. Patty, who guessed what was troubling her cousin, took her aside before preparation for a few minutes' private talk.

"Never mind telling about the Cæsar translation, Muriel," she said. "I don't care in the least. No one believes now that it was mine, and you'd never do such a thing again, I know; so what does it matter to whom it belonged? It's quite an old story now."

"I've told Miss Harper already," said Muriel, "and all the class will know about it to-morrow. Yes, Patty, I'd rather, thank you, I would indeed."

"Then I shall go to Miss Harper," declared Patty, who wished to save her cousin the humiliation of a public confession. "You shan't do this on my account!"

To her surprise, Miss Harper took quite a different view of the matter.

"No, Patty," she said, decisively. "It is generous of you to want to spare Muriel, but it is only right that she should bear the blame of what she has done herself, instead of leaving it on another's shoulders. She is making a very big effort, and we must not spoil her sacrifice. If she clears your reputation before all the class, she will have made what reparation she can, and have taken a first step on the straight path. It is not always wise to shield people from the consequences of their own faults, however much we may wish to, and you will be doing her a greater kindness by helping her to keep certain good resolutions she has made. I hope this affair may make a crisis in Muriel's life, and that we may expect better things from her in the future. I am sure she is truly sorry for having allowed you to be misjudged. Just at first, I confess, I myself believed you to be guilty, though it was difficult to reconcile your ownership of the book with what I knew of you. Various circumstances, however, caused me to change my opinion, and I was convinced that a great injustice had been done to you, which I shall now be very glad to have the opportunity of setting right."

When the girls, therefore, were assembled on the following morning at nine o'clock, Miss Harper, before she dismissed the lower division, said that she wished to speak a few words to the whole class.

"You will all recollect," she began, "a distressing affair which took place last term. A translation of Cæsar was found by a monitress in this room, and I had reason to believe it was the property of a member of the upper division. Though we mentioned no names at the time, suspicion attached itself strongly to one girl, who has since borne the blame of the occurrence. I am glad to be able to assure you that this girl was perfectly innocent. The real offender has confessed her fault, and now wishes to tell you how sorry she is for the unworthy part which she has played. Yes, it is on Muriel's behalf I am speaking," she continued, as the latter quietly left her seat and came, with a pale face, to stand by the teacher's side. "I think you will all appreciate the attempt she is making to atone for the wrong which she has done, and that instead of reproaching her you will allow the subject to drop, and will unite in keeping up such a high standard for the future, that the reputation of the Fourth Class may equal that of any other at The Priory. You may return to your place, Muriel, and I will trust to your school-fellows' honour to treat your confession with the consideration it deserves."

Miss Harper did not appeal to the class in vain. Though several girls congratulated Patty privately, none mentioned the matter in Muriel's hearing, or made any alteration in their behaviour to her. It was evident that the cousins were now on very different terms with one another, and Patty had so won all hearts that, with the exception of Vera, everybody was delighted at the change.

"I always knew Muriel would be nice to you in the end," said Avis. "All the girls who were nasty have come round, even Kitty Harrison and Maud Greening. Ella Johnson told me how you stopped her and Doris and May from reading in bed, and how thankful they were afterwards to you, when Beatrice Wynne was found out at the same thing, and got into such terrible trouble. The only one who holds back is Vera, and that's because she's so jealous of Muriel; but I don't believe Muriel will ever be really friends with her again: she can't forgive her for what happened on the shore at Moorcliffe. She says Vera ran away and left her to be drowned, and you stayed and saved her life. I hardly expect they'll have a bedroom together next term."

"I don't want them to quarrel on my account," said Patty. "I've nothing against Vera."

"Well, whether she likes you or not doesn't matter," said Enid. "I think you're the sweetest girl I've ever met, and I don't mind telling anybody so if they ask for my opinion. No, you needn't blush, because it's quite true, and everyone else in the school would say the same."

It was now getting very near to the end of the term, and all at The Priory were beginning to look forward to the long summer holidays. Speech Day, always a great occasion, was this year to be of more than usual importance, as the prizes were to be distributed by Sir John Carston, the Member of Parliament for the County, whose wife was also to be present.

"And of course hosts of parents and friends," said Enid, "to clap and look pleased and say pretty things about us. My mother and my eldest sister are coming, and Avis's father and mother, and Winnie's aunt, and ever so many relations of other girls. They're to stay at the Queen's Hotel, and they'll have quite a jolly time, I expect. They're allowed to invite us to afternoon tea there the day before, if they like, so I shall get Mother to ask you with me, if none of your own people will be over."

"I'm afraid my father and mother will be too busy to come," said Patty, "but I believe Muriel expects Uncle Sidney and Aunt Lucy."

"Then they are sure to ask you, so I shan't have a chance after all. What a pity! I wanted you to meet Mother and Adeline. Never mind! It doesn't matter, because—— But that's a secret."

"What's a secret?" enquired Patty.

"I shan't tell. Yes, I think I must. I really can't keep it bottled up any longer. I wrote home to ask Mother if she would invite you to come and stay with us during the holidays."

"Perhaps she won't want me."

"I'm sure she will. She hasn't had time to answer my letter yet, but I know she'll say 'Yes' at once, especially when she's seen you. Would you come, dear?"

"I'd love to," said Patty, "if they say 'Yes' at home too."

"Oh, I hope they will! We'd have the most glorious time together. You've never been in Devonshire, and our house is close to the sea. We bathe every day in summer, and swim out to a little rocky island sometimes. Then we go for picnics on the moors, and have gipsy teas in the woods. It's such fun to light a fire, and boil the kettle ourselves. And we have two little rough ponies; one belongs to the boys, but I could borrow a side-saddle for it from the Rectory, and then we could both go for a ride together."

"Oh, it would be delightful!" said Patty, her eyes shining at the prospect. "But I don't think you ought to have told me yet, when I haven't really been invited."

"It doesn't matter, because I'm sure you will be. I've told Mother so much about you. Oh, I wish the term would end quickly, and the holidays would begin!"

The prize-giving was held in the gymnasium, which was the only room at The Priory capable of accommodating all the classes and the various friends invited to attend. The walls were hung with flags, and beautiful vases of flowers were placed on the window sills to give an air of festivity to the scene. Patty felt there was something very inspiriting in the fact that she was a member of such a large community. She was only one amongst many, it is true, but units make numbers, and, as Miss Lincoln often reminded the girls, each had her own place to fill, and must try to do her best for the sake of the whole school.

"I'm afraid I shan't win any credit for the Upper Fourth," thought Patty. "I haven't a chance of a single prize, I know. Winnie's sure to get the first English, and Enid the second, and either Beatrice or Maggie will take the French, and perhaps the mathematics too. My exam. papers weren't very good; I'm sure I shall be quite halfway down the class. Well, never mind! As long as I haven't failed in anything, I don't much care. Father and Mother will be satisfied, because they'll know I've done as well as I could."

Although she did not expect to receive a prize, Patty nevertheless took her seat in the gymnasium on the important afternoon in question with as great interest as any other girl in the class. The platform was decorated with palms and large ferns in pots; there was a table in the middle of it, upon which were laid a number of books; and there were chairs for Miss Lincoln, Sir John and Lady Carston, and a few others of the more distinguished visitors. The proceedings, which were to consist of both concert and prize-giving combined, opened with a short speech from Miss Lincoln, welcoming the guests, and explaining briefly the principal aims which she strove to carry out in her plan of education at The Priory. A part-song followed from eight of the best girls in the singing class, among whom was Avis, who had a remarkably sweet voice, and whose high notes were as clear as a bell. Phyllis Chambers and Marjory Gregson acted a dialogue in German, some of the most advanced French scholars gave a scene from *Les Femmes Savantes,* and Enid recited the famous soliloquy from *Hamlet,* which was much applauded. With one or two more songs and piano pieces, and a solo on the violin from a girl in the lowest class, the programme for the concert was completed; and Sir John Carston then rose to address the school. He was an amusing speaker, and made all smile by assuring them he felt more nervous at facing an audience of so many young ladies than he would have been in Parliament, or at a meeting of his constituents; and that he hoped none of them were criticising his words from a literary standpoint, and comparing them with the passages from Molière and Shakespeare which had just been so admirably rendered.

"Everybody will tell you," he proceeded, "that your schooldays are the best time of your life. When I was a boy, I always thought that the best part of my schooldays was the breaking-up day! I don't know whether the teachers will agree with me, but I expect you girls will, and perhaps even Miss Lincoln may be secretly looking forward to to-morrow, though she won't reveal her feelings! I'm afraid from this you'll guess that I must have been a dunce at school myself. I frankly confess I never gained a prize in my life, but for that reason I shall appreciate all the more my privilege of distributing these beautiful books; and you will feel you have my true sympathy when I wish you a happy holiday and a long one."

Everyone laughed as Sir John sat down; the girls hoped he would have said a little more, but the time was limited, and Miss Lincoln was waiting to read out the examination lists. The awards in the Upper Fourth fell very much as Patty had expected: Winnie was first and Enid second in English, Beatrice Wynne was easily top in French, but, to everyone's surprise, Ella Johnson was head in mathematics. When all the prizes had been given, and the fortunate owners had returned to their places, Lady Carston stood up, and announced that she should like to say a few words.

"By Miss Lincoln's permission," she began, "I am going to offer an extra prize; the conditions for gaining it are to be quite different from those for which you have already competed. I wish to present it to whichever girl shall be judged by her companions to have been the most kind, the most thoughtful and generous, and to have passed the most unselfish life amongst you during the whole of the school year. The voting is to be by ballot. Each of you will be given a small piece of paper, on which I shall ask you to write the name of the one whom you consider the fittest to receive my prize. Do not add your own signature, and please do not tell anyone afterwards for whom you decided; let it be a point of honour with you to keep that matter a secret. The papers must be folded, and will then be collected by some of your teachers, who have kindly promised to count the votes. Let me mention again: I do not ask you to choose your favourite friend, or the most popular girl in your class, but the one who, you really think, has made the greatest effort towards living at the highest possible level, and whose conduct you can most honestly admire as the truest and best."

There was a rustle of astonishment among the girls at the conclusion of Lady Carston's speech. No such prize had been offered before at The Priory, and the novelty of the idea rather appealed to them. Half-sheets of notepaper were handed round by Miss Hall and Miss Rowe, and Miss Lincoln announced that five minutes would be allowed for consideration, at the end of which time the votes must be recorded. As each girl sat with her pencil in her hand, the thoughts of all turned to Patty. Everybody remembered some helpful little act which she had done, some kind thing which she had said, or an occasion when she had given up her own way to please someone else. It was not only in the Upper Fourth that she was appreciated, but among those who had met her at games, during walks, or in recreation, where, without any conscious effort on her part, her influence had had its effect on the girls, who somehow felt the better for having known her. As Enid said afterwards in strictest confidence to Avis:

"Patty isn't the least scrap of a prig. She never preaches or finds fault with one, and she's just as jolly as ever she can be; and yet she always makes one feel ashamed if one isn't doing what's absolutely straight. I've never seen her play a nasty, mean trick, nor heard her say anything horrid or unkind since she came; and if Lady Carston wanted to find out the nicest girl in the school, she couldn't fix on anybody better than Patty."

By the end of the five minutes all the papers were folded and passed back to Miss Rowe, who retired with Miss Hall to count them, while the singing class filled in the time with another part-song. There was much excitement when the two teachers returned, and handed the result to Miss Lincoln and to Lady Carston. The latter rose at once.

"I am glad to be able to tell you," she announced, "that the decision has been almost unanimous. With the exception of only three votes, every girl has recorded the same name. To Patty Hirst, therefore, I award this prize, feeling sure that I do so at the wish of the whole school. Come here, my dear," she continued, as the surprised and blushing Patty was led to the platform by Miss Rowe. "You must accept this copy of Ruskin's *Sesame and Lilies*; it is a book that I think you will like some day, when you are older, even if you cannot quite understand it now. Those who go through life with a pleasant smile and a kind word make many friends, and are always welcome visitors. Sympathy and helpfulness may be very everyday virtues, but they are worth cultivating just as much as French and mathematics, and I am sure all your companions will join with me in saying, 'Well done!'"

As Patty walked back to her seat, Lady Carston's words were answered by a perfect storm of clapping from the girls, who were delighted to have an opportunity of showing their approval; and I think no prize could have been offered which would have given more general satisfaction. As for Patty, she could still hardly realize why she had been singled out for so much notice. It was pleasant to hear her friends' congratulations, but what she valued most of all was the squeeze of the hand which Muriel gave her, with the whispered words: "I'm so glad, Patty; I can't tell you how glad!" To fulfil her promise to Uncle Sidney had been the aim of her strivings, but to have won her cousin's affection as well was more than she had ever dared to hope for.

"You needn't look so bashful!" said Enid. "You're our pattern girl at The Priory, and I don't mind telling you so. There's not the slightest fear of spoiling you, and making you vain, so it won't do you any harm for once to hear our true opinion of you."

"Oh, don't! Please don't!" cried Patty. "The prize shouldn't have been given to me. You ought each to have had one as well, you ought indeed! It's quite ridiculous to make such an absurd fuss over me, and I can't imagine why you should."

But I think most of my readers will agree that Patty deserved it.